CW01619892

ALSO BY P.F. FORD

SLATER AND NORMAN MYSTERIES
Book 1: Death By Carpet
Book 2: Death By Plane
Book 3: Death By Night
Book 4: Death By Kitchen Sink
Book 5: Death By Telephone Box
Book 6: Death In Wild Boar Woods
Book 7: Death In The River
Book 8: Death In A Skip
Book 9: Death Of A Pensioner
Book 10: Death Of A Long-Lost Son
Book 11: Death By Takeaway
Book 12: Death By Caravan

THE WEST WALES MURDER MYSTERIES
Prequel: A Date With Death
Book 1: A Body On The Beach
Book 2: A Body Out At Sea
Book 3: A Body Down The Lane
Book 4: A Body At The Farmhouse
Book 5: A Body In The Cottage
Book 6: A Body Under The Bridge

DEATH BY CARAVAN

P.F. FORD

A Slater & Norman Mystery Book 12

JOFFE BOOKS

Revised edition 2024
Joffe Books, London
www.joffebooks.com

First published as *Wrongly Convicted* in Great Britain in 2018

This paperback edition was first published
in Great Britain in 2024

© P.F. Ford 2018, 2024

This book is a work of fiction. Names, characters, businesses, organizations, places and events are either the product of the author's imagination or are used fictitiously. Any resemblance to actual persons, living or dead, events or locales is entirely coincidental. The spelling used is British English except where fidelity to the author's rendering of accent or dialect supersedes this. The right of P.F. Ford to be identified as author of this work has been asserted in accordance with the Copyright, Designs and Patents Act 1988.

Cover art by Dee Dee Book Covers

ISBN: 978-1-83526-761-5

To my amazing wife, Mary — sometimes we need someone else to believe in us before we really believe in ourselves. None of this would have happened without her unfailing belief and support.

CHAPTER ONE

It was ten a.m. on Monday morning. Norman Norman was sitting at his desk, staring out of the window at the grey, lifeless day outside. A carefully folded newspaper before him exposed a neglected crossword puzzle with just two clues filled in. This was fast becoming his daily routine, and he was beginning to wonder if maybe his former partner Dave Slater had been correct when he had suggested months ago that they might struggle to find enough work.

The only jobs he had managed to secure so far were precisely the sort he had promised himself he was never going to take: spying on supposedly errant husbands. On the plus side, he was being paid for his services, and unless someone was to knock on the door and offer to pay him to twiddle his thumbs, he had little choice but to temporarily compromise his principles. But Norman had a dream, and he was sure the work would come. It was just a question of time.

As if on cue, there was a knock on the door, and it opened just enough for a woman to peer around it. 'I'm looking for the detectives,' she said.

Norman made a point of looking around the room before he answered. 'I guess that must be me.' He jumped to his feet, walked across to the door and swung it open.

'Please, come on in,' he said with a smile. He offered his hand. 'Norman Norman, at your service.'

She shook his hand and walked into the office, her eyes nervously darting back and forth.

'There's only me here,' he said.

'Pardon?'

'You look as if you're expecting someone else to appear.'

'It says "Slater and Norman" on the door.'

'That's right,' said Norman. 'Dave Slater's my partner, but he's not here right now.'

'Oh.' Her disappointment was palpable. 'I was told there would be two of you.'

'He's out right now, but he'll be back soon.'

Slater was actually in Thailand that morning, as he had been for several weeks, but Norman thought sometimes a little white lie was needed here and there, and he was fairly confident Slater would return at some stage.

'Take a seat,' he said, indicating two armchairs with a small table between them. He followed across the room and lowered himself into the chair opposite hers. The visitor was carrying an impressive shoulder bag, which she placed carefully by the side of her chair before she sank into the soft cushions.

'I didn't catch your name,' he said.

'Debbie,' she said. 'Debbie Thomas.'

'Okay, Mrs Thomas, how can I help you?'

'Call me Debbie. I stopped being Mrs a long time ago.'

Norman waited for her to continue, but instead she stared down at her hands. She seemed to have run out of words.

'I don't want to seem in a rush,' said Norman, 'but I can't help you if you don't tell me what the problem is.'

She tried to stand up, but it was a struggle to free herself from the chair, and she didn't seem to have the energy to fight it. 'I'm sorry. I shouldn't have come. I probably can't afford you anyway.'

Norman reached across and placed a restraining hand on her arm. 'Hold on a minute,' he said, gently. 'You must have felt you had good reason to come or you wouldn't be here.'

She stopped struggling against the chair, and for the first time, she looked him right in the eye, and he could see the weariness deep within her.

'I don't know why you came here, Debbie, but I've been around long enough to know you need to talk to someone about something. I don't charge for a first consultation, and I know a thing or two about confidentiality, so now you're here, why don't you talk to me?'

She stared at him, absently biting her lip as she thought.

'If you'd prefer,' said Norman, 'I can call my girlfriend, Jane. She's great at handling more delicate stuff.'

'No, it's not like that,' she said. 'It's not about me. It's about my brother.'

'Okay. So, tell me about your brother. What's his name?'

'His name is Steve Harris. He's been in prison for ten years for something he didn't do.'

'What is he supposed to have done?'

'He was accused of murdering his wife, but he didn't do it.'

Norman wasn't expecting an answer quite like that, but he was professional enough not to show it. 'You seem very sure of that,' was all he said.

'He couldn't have done it. He just wouldn't, and anyway, he was with another woman a hundred miles away from where she died.'

'That's quite an alibi. So how come he got convicted?'

'Because the other woman denied she was with him, and someone said they saw his car near the scene of the crime.'

'Ah, right,' said Norman. 'I can see how that would complicate things. Do you know why she denied it?'

'She lied so her husband wouldn't find out where she had been.'

'Surely the police must have had other evidence to build a case?'

'It was all circumstantial. The thing is, Steve's marriage was in trouble. Everyone knew. There had been more than one big argument in public. I believe that counted against Steve so much that he was the only real suspect.'

'And his car was seen near the scene,' Norman reminded her. 'That's pretty incriminating, and it makes his alibi pretty hard to believe even if the other woman hadn't denied it.'

'You sound just like them,' she snapped. 'Steve was the husband, they were having problems. Therefore, he must be guilty.'

'That's not what I meant, although you need to understand that husbands are often the first suspects because, statistically, wives get murdered by their husbands more often than by strangers. And if his car was nearby, and he had no alibi . . .'

'But what if his alibi had come forward to say she lied all those years ago? You'd think that would make a difference, wouldn't you?'

'She's come forward? It's a bit late now, but it should be worth an appeal at least,' said Norman.

Debbie shook her head. 'It's not quite like that. She didn't come forward. She had cancer and confessed to a priest before she died.'

'She's dead?'

'I'm afraid so. The priest came and told me.'

'Isn't a confession supposed to be confidential?'

'He said some things couldn't stay confidential, especially when a man is wrongfully in prison.'

Norman puffed out a breath. 'Has he spoken to the police?'

'He won't. He says he's done his duty by speaking to me, but the police say they won't accept it second-hand from me, and the defence won't risk an appeal unless they can get the priest in the witness box.'

'And he won't do it?'

'He's gone missing. No one knows where he is, or if they do know, they won't say.'

Norman pursed his lips as he thought. 'Do you think the confession was for real?'

'What would she gain by lying when she's about to die?'

Norman nodded. 'Fair comment, but why didn't she come forward before? Why wait all this time?'

'She told Steve she didn't want her husband to find out, and he stopped saying she was with him after that.'

'And she was prepared to let him go down for murder? Jeez, she must have been some piece of work.'

'Yes, you could say that,' Debbie agreed.

'And what about the car?' asked Norman. 'That's a powerful piece of evidence, don't you think?'

'Steve swears he never drove down there. He says he couldn't drive it anywhere because he was waiting to have his brakes repaired.'

'So how was his number plate seen?' asked Norman.

'I have no idea,' she said, bitterly. 'That's why I need help.'

Norman considered for a few seconds. 'Let me be honest with you, Debbie,' he began. 'If your brother's alibi is dead, and the priest has vanished, we have no way of offering an alternative scenario even if we could prove the car wasn't there. I don't see how I'm going to be able to help, and I won't take your money just for the sake of it.'

'When I realised the confession wouldn't be any good without proof, I managed to get a newspaper to do an article about my brother. It was my last resort. The thing is, someone read the article and contacted me,' she said. 'He claims to know someone who was boasting about being paid fifty thousand pounds to kill a woman in a caravan.'

Norman sat forward in his chair. 'What exactly do you mean, he claims to know someone?'

'He did six months in prison, and while he was in there, his cellmate confessed to having been paid to kill a woman in a caravan ten years ago.'

'Let me guess — the police say he's not a credible witness,' said Norman.

She nodded. 'They warned me to expect more than one con man to come along offering information for money, and it turns out the man in question was guilty of fraud.'

'I'm afraid ex-cons always have something of a "credible witness" problem,' explained Norman, 'and being inside for fraud makes it worse. I can understand where the police are coming from.'

'The defence team won't take it any further without more proof,' added Debbie. 'That's why I'm hoping you can help me.'

'So where is this guy?' asked Norman. 'Does he have a name?'

'His name is Peter Brooks.'

'And how much is he demanding for his information?'

Debbie sighed. 'You sound just like the police again, but what if he's telling the truth? He says he doesn't want a penny.'

'You truly believe your brother is innocent, don't you?' asked Norman.

'Yes, I do. I always have. I know Steve's not perfect, Mr Norman, but he's no murderer. Will you help me?'

Norman considered again. He had to admit, he was intrigued by the story, and there was no denying the sincerity behind her belief that her brother was innocent. And let's face it, he wasn't exactly overloaded with work right now, was he?

'Having the car seen in the area is going to be a big problem,' he said, finally, 'but I am intrigued by your story. I'll tell you what I'll do — if you can give me some details about the police officers involved, I might be able to pull a few strings and get hold of the case files. I'll also see what I can find out about Peter Brooks.'

She reached down for the bag at her side and lifted it onto her lap. 'I was hoping you might be interested,' she said, rummaging in the bag, 'so I have some stuff that might help.' She produced three folders from the bag. 'Steve's defence team weren't prepared to spend any money to get this investigated, but one of the secretaries took pity on me. She made copies of the evidence the police put forward at the trial, the trial transcript, and just about everything else they have. I've also added a file of my own stuff: newspaper cuttings, photographs, the name of the priest and his last known whereabouts, and the email from Peter Brooks.'

Norman couldn't stop the broad smile that spread across his face.

* * *

Norman yawned expansively, leaned back in his chair, and stretched. He looked at the clock and was surprised to find it was after five p.m. He had spent the entire day at his desk studying the information Debbie Thomas had left with him, and he had been so engrossed he hadn't realised how late it was.

It felt good to be back in the old routine: sifting through information, looking for clues. At last, he had a real case to investigate, and for the first time in weeks, he felt the old buzz of excitement about his work. Maybe this would be the one that opened a few doors for him.

He wanted to get started right away, but experience told him now would be a good time to close the files, shut down for the day, and go home. He would sleep on it tonight, let his subconscious mull it all over, and then start again in the morning.

Carefully, he placed everything back in the correct folders and then stacked them neatly to one side of his desk. He sat back and admired the orderliness of it. Being neat and tidy was a new experience for Norman, and as it didn't come naturally to him, it was what you might call a work in progress.

It was a habit he had been encouraged to develop by Jane Jolly, his girlfriend. Jane had three children, and she had made it clear to Norman that if he was going to become part of their lives, he had to be prepared to do his share of keeping things tidy. For someone as naturally untidy as Norman, this should have been the ultimate challenge, but the truth was he was happy to do anything that would make her happy.

Now he was in his fifties, Norman felt the idea of having a 'girlfriend' didn't quite sound right, but what else should he call her? Maybe 'partner' would be more appropriate, but then he didn't want it to appear he was taking her for granted. Although he had been spending a lot of time with her, it was still early days, and he was trying desperately hard to get things right.

He was about to shut down his computer when he realised there was an email waiting in his inbox. He wondered how long it had been there and, as he was about to close up for the night, he thought about ignoring it, but curiosity got the better of him. He clicked the icon and leaned forward to see who the sender was. To his surprise, it was from Dave Slater, and for a moment he thought again about leaving it until the morning.

He had become increasingly irritated with Slater, who, apart from two or three vague emails, had kept Norman in the dark about what he was doing and what his plans were. Norman was living in Slater's house when he wasn't at Jane's house, but what was he supposed to do if Jane asked him to move in with her? He wasn't even sure if Slater intended to come back.

Then he felt guilty as he recalled how Slater hadn't even hesitated for a moment when Norman had needed somewhere to stay, and who had been there for him when he'd had his heart attack? Slater, of course. Okay, so the guy could be impetuous, but whenever Norman had been in trouble, he was always the first one there beside him, ready to drop everything and help. Guiltily, he opened the message.

Are you free tonight? My flight arrives Gatwick at 23.00. Can you pick me up? If not, no problem, let me know, and I'll hire a car.

For a moment, Norman wondered how Slater had managed to send an email from mid-air, then noticed the message had been sitting in his inbox, unnoticed, since eleven o'clock that morning. He wondered how he had managed to miss it, but then realised that was what happens when you turn off the notification sounds on your computer. Maybe silencing those annoying beeps wasn't such a good idea, after all.

'And so the wanderer returns,' he muttered. 'I suppose I'll have to go and pick him up.'

In truth, Norman hated the nights when he didn't see Jane and the kids, and being Monday, this was one of those nights, so he was actually pleased to have something to do tonight. Plus, he had to admit he had missed Slater.

Norman shut down his computer, switched off the lights, locked up the office, and climbed into his car. As he put the car into gear, he realised he was smiling, and he was whistling too.

CHAPTER TWO

It was only as he reached Gatwick Airport and parked his car that it occurred to Norman Slater's car should be here somewhere. It would be in one of the long-term car parks, but even so, if he did have a car here, why would he need picking up? As he walked across to the terminal, Norman hoped this wasn't going to be a wasted journey. If he had come all the way up here for nothing, he would be seriously annoyed.

At this time of night, the airport was relatively quiet, and he knew there wouldn't be the usual daytime crowds of people waiting for arriving passengers. He stopped to buy a coffee, then made his way to the seating area, from where he could watch the arrivals. He reasoned this was the right approach to take as he was supposed to be irritated with Slater and shouldn't appear too keen to see him.

As the clock ticked on and the time approached when Norman expected his friend to appear, he began to watch the arriving passengers more closely. At first, they arrived in ones and twos, but after a while, the numbers swelled as they all cleared customs together. Among them, a well-tanned woman with short bleached-blonde hair caught his eye. For a moment, his instincts told him he should know her, and on another day, he may well have paid her a bit more attention, but then he remembered he was here to meet his friend, not admire passing women.

It was another fifteen minutes before a deeply tanned man with a scruffy beard and straggly hair emerged. He was wearing a T-shirt, shorts and flip-flops, and was dragging a suitcase behind him. It was only when the man stopped to gaze around and then waved to him that Norman recognised him.

Before he had left England, Slater had remarked on going to 'the promised land', and ever since, Norman had harboured a fear that maybe he was going off to join a cult of some sort. Looking at Slater now, he thought perhaps he had been right to be concerned, but despite his friend's wild appearance, there was no doubting the sincerity of his greeting, and the hug was long and heartfelt. When he finally let go, Norman took a step back and looked him up and down.

'Come on, then, let's hear it,' said Slater. 'I suppose you're going to tell me I've let myself go.'

'Actually, I was thinking how well you were looking. I'm not sure about the beard, but I wouldn't mind looking half as fit and healthy.'

'I'll take that, Norm, but you don't look so bad yourself. Being with Jane must be good for you.'

Norman smiled shyly. 'I have to admit, it does add a bit of a spring to my step,' he agreed. 'I can't help noticing you're not exactly dressed for February in England, are you?'

Slater gave him a wry smile. 'It was thirty degrees when I left Thailand. I had intended to get changed before we landed, but I got distracted, and then it was too late.'

'Distracted? That sounds intriguing.'

'It's a long story,' said Slater. 'You had to be there.'

Norman watched his face for a clue, but Slater stared back blankly. He wasn't going to elaborate.

'I should warn you — it's freezing out there,' said Norman. 'Do you have anything more suitable to wear?'

'I have some jeans in my case if you don't mind waiting while I change.'

'Another five minutes won't matter. I have nothing to rush back for tonight.'

A few minutes later, they were heading for the car park.

'So how come you needed me to collect you? I thought your car was up here in long-term parking.'

He could see the discomfort on Slater's face. 'Ah, yeah, it was,' he said, vaguely.

'But it's not now?'

'Er, no.'

'Has it been stolen?'

'No. Watson landed at Gatwick without a car. She asked me if she could borrow mine to get home.'

Watson, aka DS Samantha Brearley, had been Slater's partner at his old job, before he had walked out.

Norman shook his head in surprise. 'You let her borrow your Range Rover?'

'It's no big deal. She's used to driving it. She often drove it when we were working together. I trust her with it.'

'Yeah, but even so. I mean, you wouldn't be so keen to let me drive it.'

'No offence, Norm, but I don't have enough fingers to count the number of dents in your car.'

Norman couldn't argue with that. He never claimed to be the world's best driver, but he knew he was on to something, and he wasn't going to let it go. He was sure he had just put two and two together, and he wanted to see what Slater was going to say.

'How did she get to Gatwick in the first place?'

'What?'

'You said she landed at Gatwick without a car. Presumably, she's been away somewhere, and the flight was to and from Gatwick. I'm curious to know how she got to Gatwick in the first place. People usually have transport arranged — they don't fly into Gatwick on the off-chance someone's going to lend them a Range Rover to get home.'

Slater stopped walking and turned to face him.

'Seriously, are you pissed off just because I let her borrow my car?'

Norman laughed. 'Of course not. Even I wouldn't lend me a Range Rover. I'm curious, that's all. I mean, how did you get the key to her? Or does she have her own? I could swear the spare is in the key drawer at home.'

He waited for a response, but Slater seemed to be struggling for words.

'And another thing,' continued Norman. 'You couldn't have emailed me from the sky, right? So, you must have known this morning that she was going to borrow your car.'

Even behind Slater's beard and the deep suntan, Norman could see his cheeks reddening. He looked away from Norman and stared up at the sky for inspiration. Norman guffawed loudly and slapped him on the shoulder.

'Don't tell me — it was an amazing coincidence, right? She landed at the same time as you, and I suppose you just happened to bump into her, and as luck would have it, you had emailed me to come and meet you just in case this should happen. Am I close?'

Slater stared at the grinning Norman and knew the game was up. 'You knew all the time, didn't you?'

'I saw a familiar face coming through arrivals,' Norman confessed as they started walking again. 'I knew I should know her, but I couldn't think who she was at the time. Then, when I asked about the car and you mentioned her name, the penny dropped. Hey, look, there's no need to be embarrassed, I'm not going to tell anyone. Has she been out there all the time?'

'God, no, she would have lost her job. She had some leave, so she came out for the last ten days.'

'You can tell me to mind my own business, but my curiosity is getting the better of me now. Has this been going on for long?'

'If you mean, was I having a relationship with my junior officer? Not at all. We were very professional while we were working together, but once I quit . . . well, that's when we told each other what we were thinking.'

'So, when you said about going to the promised land that day—'

'I wasn't talking about Thailand. That came after.'

'What happens now?'

'She's gone back to start a new job, and I've come home.'

'And that's it?' asked Norman. 'You let her take your car, and you don't even know if you'll see her again?'

Slater smiled. 'Yeah, I guess that's about the size of it. It's just a car, Norm. Anyway, I trust her. I know she'll get it back to me in one piece.'

'Yeah, but when?'

'I dunno,' Slater admitted. 'Whenever it gets here, I guess. And just so you know, you haven't uncovered some big, secret romance.'

'I haven't?'

'We're just two consenting adults who fancied spending a few days together, with no strings attached.'

They had reached the car now, and as they loaded Slater's case into the boot, Norman shook his head. 'And that's it? You spend ten nights with a beautiful woman and then you go your separate ways?'

'It's not that hard to understand, Norm. Sam's a career girl, and no one is going to get in the way of that.'

'What about you?'

Slater gave a wry smile. 'Have you ever known me keep a relationship going for long?'

'Jeez, I don't think I'll ever understand you and women.'

'Ha! I've never been able to, Norm, so what makes you think you can?'

* * *

As they headed back towards Tinton, Slater listened as Norman told him about his developing relationship with Jane Jolly and her three children. Norman was happier than Slater had ever seen him, and he was immensely pleased for his friend. If any couple deserved to be together, it was Norm and Jane. They'd been through some crappy times through no fault of their own, and he genuinely wished them the best.

'Hey, listen to me,' said Norman, about an hour into the journey. 'I've done nothing but talk, and you can't get a word in anywhere.'

'It's good to hear you sounding happy,' said Slater. 'I'm pleased it's all working out for you and Jane on the romantic front, but what are you doing for work?'

Now Norman felt uncomfortable. He had been hoping they might avoid that subject, at least until the morning. 'Remember that office we were cleaning up? Well, I finally got one room finished and opened for business.'

'As a detective?'

Norman wasn't sure if he could hear any sarcasm in the question. 'Yeah, as a detective. What else would I be doing?'

'Have you got much work?'

'I'm getting by,' said Norman, vaguely.

Slater looked across at him. 'You mean you haven't got any work, right?'

This was definitely without sarcasm. 'I could give you a load of bullshit, but I'll be honest and admit I haven't had any real detective work. In fact, the only job I've been working the last couple of weeks is one I'd rather not have — spying on some guy whose wife thinks he's cheating on her.'

Slater grimaced. 'And is he?'

'Not that I can see,' said Norman, 'but she insists I've got to keep following him and she keeps on paying . . .'

'You always said you wouldn't take jobs like that.'

'I seem to recall we both said it,' Norman reminded him, 'but it's a necessary evil. I have to make money somehow. Even though I don't eat anywhere near the amount of food I used to, I can't live on fresh air.'

'I said it would be like that,' Slater told him, but again there didn't seem to be any hint of smugness.

'Yeah, I know, but I'm sure if I'm prepared to put up with a few crappy jobs to start with, the good stuff will find its way to me in the end,' said Norman. 'Anyway, enough about my work. What are you going to do now you're back?'

'I have no idea. I've burnt my bridges with the police, that's for sure.'

'Walking out the first time was risky,' agreed Norman, 'but doing it the second time certainly wasn't your finest hour. I know you were upset, but maybe you should have waited for the dust to settle first.'

'I wouldn't want to go back again, Norm. It was a mistake going back last time. I've always believed right is right and wrong is wrong, but the older I've got, the more I find I have to compromise my principles to do my job. Bad people get away with bad things far too often for my liking, and as a police officer, I just had to sit back and let them get away with it. Even when we know they're guilty, we have to let them free on some stupid technicality, and they laugh in our faces as they walk out! I've done a lot of soul-searching while I've been away, and I know I can't work like that again.'

'I get where you're coming from, but I don't think there's a vacancy for Superman right now,' said Norman.

Slater smiled. 'Just as well, really. I've never felt comfortable wearing my underwear on the outside. It's not a look that suits me.'

'But seriously, what are you going to do?'

'I'll think of something.'

'You could come and work with me,' suggested Norman.

Slater looked across at him. 'I thought you said you only had one job.'

'Yeah, well, I've been looking at another one today, and I think it may be the one I've been waiting for.'

'I'm not sure spying on cheating husbands is my thing.'

'This isn't about spying on anyone.'

'I don't know, Norm . . .'

'Look, if this is because of me being selfish, I promise you I've changed. And you won't believe how tidy I have had to become to keep Jane happy.'

'When did I ever complain about you being selfish?' asked Slater.

'You didn't,' said Norman, 'but when I was working with Naomi, she pointed it out to me. She told me how I always used to leave you to do all the paperwork and crap that I don't like doing. She said I was selfish, and it must drive you mad, but you wouldn't complain because you're you. She said you went back to the police because you didn't want to work with me.'

'I went back to the police because I was an idiot,' said Slater, grimly.

Norman wasn't sure how to respond to that and settled for saying nothing.

'You did tend to leave me to do the crap,' admitted Slater, 'but it never stopped me wanting to work with you. I can honestly say I enjoyed working with you, I always did.'

'So why don't we start again? Only this time I'll do my fair share, and if I don't, you'll let me know.'

'I thought you and Naomi were a team.'

'We were, sort of, but when that homeless kid got killed, she took it badly. She felt it was her fault. Now she's decided she can't do it anymore.'

'I thought she wanted to make a difference.'

'Yeah, but didn't we all at one time? She still does want to make a difference, but now she thinks she can do more good by working with people who need help, like the homeless.'

Slater nodded his approval. 'She's probably right. Maybe I should do something like that.'

'The point is, Naomi's out of the picture, so what do you say?' asked Norman.

Slater thought about it. 'But if you're getting together with Jane you're going to need the money, Norm. It wouldn't be right for me to come barging in now, not after you've spent money and done all the work getting things set up for yourself.'

Norman felt his face begin to redden. 'Ah, yeah, well, that's where it gets a little embarrassing,' he said, sheepishly. 'The thing is, I haven't exactly spent any money. The business remains "Slater and Norman", and I'm using the stationery we had printed that says the same thing. I was going to get it changed once I started to make some money.'

Slater laughed at Norman's discomfort. 'And you were worried about telling me that?'

'Well, I thought maybe you wouldn't want your name to be associated—'

'Jesus, Norm, I've never been embarrassed to be associated with you. Why would I? You're my best mate, for God's sake. If anything, I'm the embarrassment, the way I go storming off in a huff every time things don't go quite how I want them to.'

'I wouldn't put it quite like that,' said Norman. 'You have principles. I understand that.'

'You don't have to dress it up, Norm — we both know I'm a forty-something who can behave like a toddler.'

Norman wasn't sure quite how he should respond to Slater's honesty, but luckily, he didn't have to.

'However, in my defence,' Slater continued, 'I've just spent several weeks learning how to be a better person, so I should be able to behave a bit more like an adult in future.'

Now it was Norman's turn to laugh. 'You're going to be an adult? You're kidding me, right? Does Watson know about this?'

Slater could see the funny side, and he was smiling too. 'Having shared a hotel room with me for two weeks, she says she likes the new, adult me even better than the old one.'

'Is she gonna be upset that I know about you and her?'

'Nice try, Norm, but you're not going to catch me out. I already told you there is no me and her. She was happy to walk through customs with me, but I was the one who suggested we shouldn't come out together because I thought it might not look good for her new job if anyone saw her with me.'

They drove on in silence for a few minutes until Norman spoke again. 'Well, while you've got nothing else to do, I could do with some help.'

'What about this guy you should be spying on?'

'They're in Portugal for three weeks, staying with her parents. She says he wouldn't dare risk messing around in front of them. And if you're worried about an early start, I don't usually start until ten. It makes up for all the times I have to work late.'

Slater grinned. 'You don't give up, do you?'

'What else have you got to do?' asked Norman. 'Why don't you sleep on it and let me know in the morning?'

CHAPTER THREE

Despite having had little sleep, Slater was intrigued by Norman's new case. As they ate breakfast, he asked questions.

'So, this convicted guy is called Steve Harris, and his story is that his wife, Julie, had arranged to go away for the weekend to see an old friend. While she was away, her sister, Jackie Smith, moved in and kept her side of the bed warm, right?'

'That's right,' said Norman, 'but at the time, the sister said that was a lie, and her husband insisted she was at home with him.'

'It was the Smiths' word against his, and that meant his alibi was toast, right?'

'To be honest, if we'd been investigating this case, we'd have thought his alibi was bullshit too,' said Norman.

'But now a priest has come forward to say the sister confessed she was lying and she was with Harris that weekend?'

'That's about the size of it.'

'And there's no forensic evidence to link Harris to the murder?'

'That's how it looks,' Norman said. 'The whole case against him relied on three things. First, the witness who claimed to have seen the car. Second, that he didn't report her missing until Monday evening. Third, the fact all their friends said they had the sort of marriage that was mostly arguments that sometimes blew up into actual fights.'

'Why didn't he report her missing?'

'He says it was because Jackie Smith was still at his house on Monday morning. He says she didn't want to go home because she was frightened of her husband.'

Slater pulled a face. 'What about Harris fighting with his wife? Was that his fault?'

'Probably. It seems our friend Mr Harris is the type of guy who regards adultery as a hobby — just like some guys go fishing, he went shagging. But his wife wasn't the sort to take that without a murmur. He openly admits he couldn't resist a pretty face and was a crap husband. On the other hand, he also claims he loved his wife and would never raise a hand to her.'

'But what about the fights?'

'Plenty of people said they argued a lot, but no one can recall Julie ever saying he had hit her, nor seeing any bruises on her. One or two of the men reckon they had seen scratches and bruises on Steve, although he never complained about her.'

'She was the violent one? That's unusual.'

'Yeah, but when that came out, it was used against him. They claimed Julie was leaving him and he followed her to try and stop her. An argument developed, she started hitting him, went too far, and he lost his temper and killed her in retaliation.'

'As a theory, I suppose it works,' said Slater. He chewed thoughtfully for a few moments. 'What do you think, Norm? What's your theory?'

'Heck, I haven't got that far yet, but we know the original case seems to hinge on the alibi or lack thereof. After hearing about the confession, you'd have to question that, right?'

'But without the priest, you've got nothing,' said Slater.

'That's true,' admitted Norman, 'but then there's this other guy who claims someone else got paid fifty thousand pounds. I know he could be spinning a line, but if I can find him and he's telling the truth, maybe we won't need the priest at all.'

Slater nodded. 'If the priest is right and the Smiths were lying about her being at home,' he mused, 'you have to wonder what they were hiding — and why? What do we know about this Smith guy?'

'Not much that I can recall,' said Norman. 'Like I said, I've still got a lot of reading to do.'

Slater grinned. 'If he's the sort of guy who knew what his wife was up to, maybe he coerced her into the lie so he could make sure Steve Harris got the blame for the murder. Maybe Smith saw it as payback for Harris messing around with Mrs Smith.'

'Jeez, d'you think so? That's one hell of a payback.'

Slater winked at him. 'It's a theory, right? It might be somewhere for us to start.'

'Us? You mean you'll help me?'

'Like you said, I've got nothing else to do, have I?'

CHAPTER FOUR

When Slater and Norman had first taken over the converted stable block a few months ago, they never quite decided how they were going to use the rooms, and because he couldn't make his mind up what would be best, Norman had chosen to decorate only the front office and keep the larger one empty. For this reason, it hadn't been finished yet, but it was now ideally suited to become their 'incident room', the off-white boards that covered the walls quite adequate for the purpose.

Slater stepped back and admired his handiwork. With all the photographs and a few notes pinned to the walls, it was beginning to look like they were running a proper investigation. Just at that moment, Norman walked in carrying two mugs of tea. He had his notebook tucked under his arm.

'Wow! It's almost like the real thing,' he said.

'I thought it might be a bit easier to follow things if we had it all laid out,' said Slater. 'We still need to join all the dots, but it's a start.'

He pointed to the photograph of Steve Harris. 'I feel I should know this guy, but I can't think why.'

'I can't help you there,' said Norman. 'If he was an old case, it was before my time. He was in prison long before I arrived on the scene.'

'It'll come to me, I'm sure,' said Slater. He pointed to a photo of Jackie Smith. 'Of course, if she were still alive this would be a bloody sight easier, but then I suppose that's exactly why we've got this case.'

Then he pointed to a photograph of a caravan. 'What do we know about this caravan?'

Norman put the teas down, joined Slater in front of the boards, and consulted his notes. 'It was owned by the company that employed Julie Harris. Apparently, it was a staff benefit. For a nominal fee, anyone could use it as long as they booked in advance.'

'And Julie had booked it?'

'It wasn't booked by anyone that weekend because the site closes down from the end of November through to the first of March. Apparently, there was maintenance work planned, but she would have known when that was due to happen.'

'Was it the maintenance team who found her?'

'The maintenance was never carried out, so it was several weeks before anyone looked inside.'

'That was convenient for whoever murdered her. Do we know why the work never happened?' Slater asked.

'I can't find anything about it. It's something we need to check out.'

'Julie was the boss's secretary, wasn't she?'

'Two guys jointly owned the company. They shared her.'

'Was there any suggestion they were . . . ?'

'According to what we know, both marriages were fine, and there was nothing to suggest anything was going on that shouldn't have been. But it was her job to keep track of the caravan bookings, so she would have known it was empty that weekend.'

'And this place is in Wales, isn't it? What's that, a four-hour drive from here?'

'About that, yeah.'

'If he'd driven there, Harris's car would have shown up on the CCTV across the Severn Bridge, wouldn't it?'

'Yeah, but they couldn't find any sign of it,' said Norman. 'Their theory was that he could easily have gone the long way around, and avoided the CCTV.'

'Bloody hell, how many hours does that add to the journey?' asked Slater. 'And did they have proof using the Automatic Number Plate Recognition cameras?'

'If they had proof, there's no mention of it here.'

'Christ, you were right when you said the case was circumstantial. You could drive a bloody bus through some of these holes.'

'If you ask me, it wasn't what the police could prove so much as what Harris's defence couldn't prove that led to his conviction.'

'What do you make of this crime scene?' Slater pointed to the photos beneath the caravan.

Norman gazed at the photographs. He hadn't had time to study them yet as he'd been reading all the written material. After a minute or so, he spoke. 'That's a very tidy crime scene if it was a fight that got out of hand.'

'Right,' agreed Slater. 'Anything else?'

'Well, if that's all the luggage they found, I'd say that's a damned small holdall to pack if she was leaving home.'

'That's what I thought. That bag would barely hold enough to last a weekend.'

'Unless you were planning on spending the weekend in bed,' added Norman.

'Exactly. I don't think Julie was leaving home for good. I think she was on a dirty weekend of her own. So who was she hoping to spend that dirty weekend with?'

'Even if we're right and she was meeting someone,' said Norman, 'it doesn't put Steve Harris in the clear. If anything, it reinforces the motive they put forward.'

'Yeah, I know,' said Slater, 'but that's not what I'm suggesting. What happened to the guy who was meeting her? Why didn't he find the body and report it? If he saw Harris arrive and kept out of his way I understand that, but why not come forward and tell the police Harris had been there?

There wouldn't be much doubt about who murdered her then, would there?'

'Perhaps he did a runner because he had a wife of his own at home?'

'But even if he didn't want to show his face, he could have made an anonymous call. And what if he didn't run away? What if he killed her?'

'Maybe he didn't show up for some reason, or perhaps you're right and it was because he was the one who killed Julie — and Steve Harris is telling the truth.'

'There you go, Norm. It's just like the old days. We're still on the same wavelength.'

'So now you're back in the saddle you're starting to enjoy yourself. See, I said you would.'

'If I thought it was going to be like this all the time, I would find it hard to say no,' admitted Slater. 'But we both know we'd be more likely to be spying on cheating spouses. I'm not sure I can handle doing that all the time.'

'Aw, come on, don't think like that,' Norman urged him. 'Who knows what might happen if we can crack this one?'

'If we're going to do this, we need to start by speaking to Steve Harris.'

'No problem. While you were sticking things to the wall in here, I made a couple of phone calls. We're going up there tomorrow morning.'

Slater's head snapped round to stare at him. Norman grinned back at him. 'Hey, don't look so surprised. I told you I was a changed man.'

Slater gave him a wry smile. 'I'm not sure I can handle all this efficiency. I suppose you've got this afternoon planned as well, have you?'

'I haven't managed to track down Peter Brooks yet, but we have to start somewhere, so I thought we might visit Julie's old workplace, as it's nearest.'

'Don't tell me you've made an appointment there as well.'

'And warn everyone we're coming? No way. I thought it would be better if we turn up unannounced and see how fast the grapevine works.'

CHAPTER FIVE

'What did you learn about Pritchard and Harkness?' Norman asked Slater as he drove away from their office.

'Not much. They started off as a couple of architects, quickly made a name for themselves, became a limited company, swallowed up a couple of small building firms, and became property developers. They're pretty big players now, doing the whole design, plan and build thing, operating at the higher end of the market. The managing director is a guy called James Harkness.'

'What about Pritchard?'

'I only had a quick scan of the website, but I didn't see that name mentioned anywhere apart from in the company name.'

'Okay, a blank slate works for me,' said Norman. 'We'll make out we know nothing and start from scratch.'

* * *

Slater knew from the website that James Harkness was in his early fifties, but when they met, he thought Harkness looked much older. He had been surprised when they had explained why they were there but had ushered them into his office without hesitation.

'I've got ten minutes before I have to leave for a site meeting,' he said, 'so I'd appreciate it if you can make it quick.'

'We have a few questions,' said Norman. 'It won't take long.'

Harkness pointed to the more comfortable chairs away from his desk. 'So, you're private investigators,' he remarked. 'It was a long time ago, you know. I'm not sure how much help I can be.'

'We realise ten years is a long time,' said Slater, 'but we're hoping a murder might not be an everyday occurrence in your life.'

Harkness gave Slater a distasteful look. He obviously wasn't a big fan of sarcasm.

'It's possible some new evidence has come to light,' explained Norman, hastily, 'and we've been asked to check it out.'

'New evidence? What sort of new evidence? I seem to recall there hadn't been much doubt who was responsible at the time. I wasn't much help back then, so I don't see how I can help so many years after the event.'

'We like to be thorough, so we thought we'd start at the beginning,' said Slater. 'It helps us get a better feel for a case.'

'You knew Julie Harris, didn't you, Mr Harkness?' asked Norman. 'Wasn't she your secretary?'

'Well, I suppose you could say that,' Harkness said. 'Although it was my business partner back then who interviewed and employed her. He was the one who knew her.'

'Your partner is Mr Pritchard, right?' asked Norman.

'Was Mr Pritchard,' corrected Harkness. 'I'm afraid he passed away five years ago.'

'Oh, I'm sorry. We had no idea. Can I ask what happened to him?'

'I'm afraid he took Julie's death very hard. He felt responsible. He started drinking very heavily, became depressed, and eventually committed suicide.'

'Why did he feel responsible?' asked Slater.

'Because he was very fond of her, and it had been his idea to buy the caravan where she died.'

'Fond of her?'

Harkness glared at Slater. 'Don't you dare try to read anything into that,' he snarled. 'John Pritchard was a happily married man who cared about his employees. I won't have his name dragged through the mud.'

'We're not here to drag anyone's name through the mud,' said Norman. 'We're just trying to understand the relationships. You just said you didn't know your secretary. Isn't that a bit odd?'

'Well, I knew who she was, of course, but what I mean is I didn't know anything about her. John was the one who was here all the time. I spent most of my time out on the road. That's how we worked in those days, you see. He was based here drawing up plans, and I was the one who went out to see clients and manage jobs.'

'But if she was your secretary—'

'I didn't see Julie very often because I used to dictate my notes at home of an evening, and she would transcribe them the next day. I used to meet up with John here at eight every morning, but I'd be gone before she started work at nine. The three of us made a very successful team, but I can't say I knew much about Julie. I was never here to spend time chatting with her.'

'Tell us about the caravan,' Norman said.

'That was John's idea. We already had a lodge up in Scotland for our own use, but he thought a static caravan down by the seaside would be an asset we could use to reward the people who worked for us.'

'Did you have that many employees?' asked Slater.

'We used to work with a lot of building contractors. The idea was to reward them with a chance to take their family away for a week in Wales.'

'Isn't that called bribery?'

Harkness gave Slater a mirthless smile. 'I think you'll find it's called business.'

'Did it get used much?' asked Norman.

'We only bought it in the spring of 2007. Julie's murder took place in January 2008. It didn't seem such a good idea after her body was found. We got rid of it as soon as we could after that.'

'But did it get used much when you had it?' Norman persisted.

'Not really. I had always had my doubts about it, but John thought it was a good idea.'

'I understand Julie used to handle the bookings, is that right?'

'Julie and John handled it between them.'

'What happened if no one was using it?' asked Slater. 'Did it sit empty?'

Harkness sighed. 'John used to go down there most weekends if it was empty. He had a thing about birdwatching. To tell the truth, I used to think that was the only reason he had wanted it in the first place.'

'Was he there the weekend Julie died?' asked Slater.

Harkness gave Slater that distasteful look again. 'If you think you can pin the murder on the dead man just to get your client off the hook, you're making a grave mistake. John was in Scotland, birdwatching.' He looked pointedly at his watch. 'Now, I'm afraid that's all the time I have.'

'No problem,' said Norman, getting to his feet. 'Thank you for sparing us your time. You've been very helpful.'

* * *

'Is it me, or did he manage to avoid telling us anything useful?' asked Norman, as they climbed back into his car.

'Oh, I don't know,' said Slater. 'He made sure to tell us nothing was his fault.'

'D'you think he was suggesting something was going on between John Pritchard and Julie Harris?'

'If you mean, was he faking the indignation? I'm not sure,' said Slater. 'It did seem to be a bit of an extreme reaction.'

'It's easy to pass the buck when the other guy's dead. I'd love to hear John Pritchard's side of the story.'

'Is his widow still around?'

'I haven't got that far.'

'I'll check it out when we get back,' said Slater. 'Maybe she'd be willing to speak to us.'

'It's worth a try.'

As Norman pulled the car into their designated parking spot, Slater glanced across to their office. A woman was standing outside, apparently waiting.

'We could do with a receptionist or something,' said Slater. 'A woman is waiting outside. We could have missed her, and she might have the big job we're waiting for.'

As Norman looked up, the woman turned in their direction. 'She has the big job we're investigating now. That's Debbie Thomas. I told her to give me twenty-four hours, and I'd let her know if I was going to take the case.'

As he saw her face, Slater sank back in his seat. 'Oh, Jesus, no wonder the name seemed so familiar,' he muttered.

'What?'

'I just remembered I have to get to the bank before they close.'

'You should have said. I could have dropped you off.'

'Like I said, I just remembered,' said Slater. 'You can handle this, can't you?'

'I was rather hoping to introduce you to Debbie,' said Norman. 'She was expecting two of us yesterday, and I fed her some crap about you being on vacation.'

'Well, feed her some more crap now,' said Slater, opening the car door and sliding out. 'I have to go, or I'll be in trouble.'

'Hang on a minute,' began Norman, but Slater was already across the car park, and Norman could only watch as he disappeared down the footpath that led towards town.

'What the hell was that about?' he muttered. As he climbed from the car and headed for the office, he pasted a professional smile on his face. 'Hi, Debbie. Boy, are you keen?'

She smiled back at him. 'You did say twenty-four hours, and that was yesterday morning.'

'You got me there,' agreed Norman.

'Was that Dave Slater?' she asked, looking across the car park in the direction Slater had fled.

'Yeah. I'm sorry, Dave had to rush off. He has some business at the bank, and he was worried they might close.'

'That's a pity. I was hoping to see him. I used to know him.'

'Oh, really? He didn't say,' said Norman.

'It was a long time ago,' she said wistfully. 'Maybe he's forgotten.'

Norman said nothing as he unlocked the office door and led her inside.

'So, what do you think?' she asked. 'Will you help me?'

'We've had a good look at your case, and I'm pleased to tell you we are going to look into it,' he told her, 'but you have to understand that we can't guarantee we'll find what you want us to find.'

'I understand that,' she said, 'but I have every confidence in you. You're my brother's last chance.'

'No pressure then,' said Norman, with a wry smile.

'I know you'll do your best. I don't ask for any more than that.'

'I can guarantee that.'

CHAPTER SIX

'Did you rush off to avoid someone, or was my imagination playing tricks on me?' asked Norman, when Slater returned a few minutes later.

'I had to go to the bank,' answered Slater, avoiding Norman's gaze.

'Call me suspicious, but I don't think you've been anywhere near the bank. In fact, I would suggest you've been hiding where you could watch the office until someone left.'

'I don't know what you mean.'

'You know perfectly well what I mean. If I had to guess, I'd say you didn't want to see Debbie Thomas. Am I right?'

Slater sighed and looked off into the distance for a moment. He kicked aimlessly at a wastepaper basket and then appeared to come to a decision.

'Yes, I knew her, but it was a long time ago, and she was Debbie Harris back then,' he said, turning to face Norman.

'Was she another one of your girlfriends?'

'It was a long time ago.'

'D'you want to talk about it?'

Slater suddenly felt the need to study his feet.

'So, she wasn't like all the others?' asked Norman.

'You could say that,' said Slater, quietly. 'Fancy a beer?'

Norman glanced at his wristwatch. 'Yeah, why not?' He patted his pockets. 'You're in luck, I've even brought my wallet along.'

* * *

Slater chose a quiet table well away from the bar.

'When I first left school, I worked in a bank,' he began, when Norman joined him with two beers.

Norman pulled a face as he sipped his pint.

'Yeah, I know, but I was just a kid, and I had no idea. I thought it would be an easy way to make a living. Anyway, Debbie came to work there, too. She was sixteen, I was eighteen, and I was asked to show her how things worked. I went to a boys' school, so I'd never really got to spend time with a girl before. I thought she was beautiful, and we just seemed to hit it off. We started dating, and two years later, I asked her to marry me.'

Norman nearly spilled his beer. 'You asked her to marry you? Oh, wow, you really were smitten.'

Slater gave a sad little smile. 'Her parents were pleased about it. I guess they thought I was the just the right steady sort of guy with a sensible career and a good future — you know the sort of thing.'

Norman nodded. Yes, he knew the sort of thing, exactly.

'We had the date set, and everything was arranged,' continued Slater, 'and then, a month before the wedding, she told me she was three months pregnant.'

Norman grimaced. 'That's not ideal, but it's not the end of the world.'

'It is when you're not the father,' said Slater grimly.

He took a long drink from his glass, creating an awkward silence that Norman felt he should fill. He should have seen this coming and wondered if there was an appropriate response to such a statement, but quickly decided that if there was, he had no idea what it would be.

'Ah,' was all he managed to say.

'She was my first girlfriend, and I was as green as grass,' said Slater. 'I mean, we used to kiss and cuddle, but I had this naive idea that it would be good to wait until we got married, and I thought she felt the same.'

There was another silence, but this time Norman resisted the temptation to fill it.

'It turns out,' said Slater, with a mirthless smile, 'she was gagging for it, and when I didn't deliver, she found someone else who was only too happy to oblige. The thing was, he'd been obliging her for over a year when I found out.'

Norman couldn't hide his disbelief. 'And she was still going through with the wedding?'

'She blamed that on me, and her parents. She claimed she just got carried along with the whole thing, and no one stopped to ask her what she thought. She reckoned she had been trying to tell me it was all over, but the time never seemed right, you know?'

'Shit.'

'Yeah, that's one word for it,' agreed Slater. 'Apparently, I was too boring. She already had a boring job, and with me, she would have had a completely boring life. She wanted some excitement in her life and cheating on me with this other guy was providing the excitement she craved.'

'Did you know the guy?' asked Norman.

Slater smiled his mirthless smile again. 'Oh, yeah, I knew him alright. He was going to be my best man!'

'Jeez, that's some story. I don't know what to say,' said Norman, hopelessly. 'What happened after that?'

'Her dad tried to force the other guy to take my place. He'd spent a fortune on the wedding already, and he was determined to get his money's worth, but Casanova did a runner, and that was the end of that.'

'So much for her exciting life,' said Norman. 'Did she keep the baby? I would imagine having a baby at nineteen would cramp your style.'

'I have no idea,' said Slater. 'I soon realised nearly everyone I knew had known what was going on. Can you imagine how that felt? I handed my notice in at the bank a couple of weeks later, left Winchester, and moved to Tinton. This is the first time I've seen Debbie since then.'

'So that's why you didn't recognise her name.'

'She was still Harris, last time I saw her,' said Slater, taking another mouthful of beer.

'If you went out with her for that long you must know her brother, right?'

'He's a couple of years older than Debbie. He was in the army back then and was away a lot. I got the impression his parents tried to run his life. The army allowed him to be himself. If I saw him more than half a dozen times I'd be surprised, and I certainly didn't get to know him.'

'Are you going to be okay taking this case?' asked Norman.

'If you mean am I over her? Yes, I am. Working the case won't be a problem.'

'I can make sure you don't have to meet up with her if you like.'

'No, don't worry. I'll be fine. I was just taken by surprise seeing her like that.'

'I'm sorry, I should have warned you.'

'Don't be daft, Norm. There was no way you could have known, and as I said, it was over twenty years ago. I'm fine.'

'Well, if it's any consolation,' said Norman, 'I know how it feels to get kicked in the teeth by a woman, but I'm not sure I would have coped if I'd been that young when it happened.'

'Oh, I really struggled with the disappointment,' said Slater, 'but looking back now, I can see she was right. I was boring. I hate to admit it, but everything about my life back then was boring and predictable. I needed a kick up the arse, and I got one. Debbie Harris is the reason I became a police officer.'

'A police officer's life is anything but predictable, that's for sure,' said Norman.

There was a brief silence while they both contemplated their beers.

'It's why I don't have many friends,' said Slater.

'Huh?'

'They all knew, and yet no one told me. I never felt so stupid in my life as when I realised they were going to let me make a mistake that could have messed up my whole life and no one was prepared to warn me. It made it really hard for me to trust anyone, and I've sort of stayed that way.'

'It also explains why you have this problem with women,' Norman added.

Slater stiffened. 'I don't have a problem with women. I've had plenty of girlfriends.'

'Yes, but none of them stick, do they? As soon as things start to get serious, you end it. I reckon, deep down, you're frightened to commit to a relationship because of what happened back then.'

Slater grinned. 'That's bollocks, Norm.'

'I think we both know it's not. I think what happened back then clouds your judgment about every woman you've met since.'

'Well, thank you for your amazing insights, Doctor Freud,' said Slater, testily, 'but I think I've heard enough now. You asked me about Debbie Thomas, and I explained. This matter is now closed. '

'Okay, okay. If that's what you want.'

'It is. And I would like it to stay that way. Now, d'you want another beer?'

Norman glanced at his watch. 'I'm sorry,' he said, guiltily. 'I said I'd be at Jane's. Can I give you a lift home?'

'No, you're okay. I'll walk. The exercise will do me good.'

CHAPTER SEVEN

Steve Harris was a big man. At six feet four, he towered over both detectives. Even sitting down, it was easy to see he would be a force to be reckoned with. As Slater and Norman sat down opposite him, he gave them an appraising look.

Harris studied Slater's face.

'My sister says you nearly married her.'

'It was a long time ago.'

'She reckons I should know you. Your face is vaguely familiar, but I can't recall us ever being friends.'

'You were in the army,' said Slater. 'I think I only saw you half a dozen times.'

'Ah, yes, that's right. The army was my escape from the old man. He wanted me to follow in his footsteps, but I had other plans. I did three years and hardly ever went home. He backed off in the end.'

Harris studied the two faces again.

'Debbie tells me you two are going to get me out of here. Is that right?'

'Let's not get ahead of ourselves,' replied Norman. 'All we agreed to do was take a look at your case. We can't make any guarantees about the outcome.'

'Does that mean you think I'm guilty?'

'It means we're only just getting started, and at this stage, we have no opinion one way or the other,' said Slater.

'That's not very reassuring.'

'It should be,' said Norman, 'because it means we're being honest with you.'

'You two are ex-coppers, aren't you?' said Harris. 'That means you're probably going to agree with the original inquiry and say I'm guilty because it's the easy thing to do, and it'll keep your old mates happy.'

Norman gave him a cold smile. 'Actually, I think you'll find neither of us have any "old mates" to keep happy. We had a habit of pissing people off because we didn't always agree with them.'

'Yeah, right,' Harris sneered.

'We're not prepared to say we'll get you out of here, because we're not in the business of making promises we can't keep,' said Norman. 'As for the original police investigation, yes, we're aware of their findings, but we prefer to conduct independent investigations and draw our conclusions from the evidence we have gathered.'

'What the hell does that mean?'

'It means we're going to start at the beginning and see where it takes us,' said Slater. 'When we've finished, we'll know who killed your wife. If it isn't you, we'll do our best to get you out of here. If it is you, well . . .'

Harris glared at Slater and slammed his fist down on the table. 'What do you mean "if it was you"? I didn't kill my wife. How many more times do I have to say it?'

'What my partner means is that we try to keep an open mind,' explained Norman. 'I'm sure you must realise if we took everyone who claimed to be innocent at face value, this prison would be empty. Right now, we're all you've got, so losing your temper isn't the best way of helping us to help you.'

Harris gave Slater another dirty look, but Norman was right. They were his only hope. 'Okay,' he said, reluctantly, 'I'll tell you whatever you want to know, but don't tell me I'm guilty, alright?'

Slater held his hands up in a sign of appeasement but didn't offer an apology.

'In your original statement, you claim you were with Jackie Smith,' he said. 'So how come your car was seen near the scene of the crime. How do you explain that?'

'I can't explain it,' said Harris. 'The witness must have been mistaken. I say that because my car was at home, in my garage, on axle stands with the back wheels off, waiting for new brake discs.'

'Did you do all your own maintenance?' asked Norman.

'Where possible. I enjoyed tinkering, lots of guys do. The parts were ordered, and I was waiting for them to arrive.'

'Yeah,' said Slater, 'the police checked. They say you didn't order them until after Julie died. You would have had time to drive to Wales and back and then remove the wheels.'

'But I didn't,' said Harris. 'The discs were wafer thin. There was no way I would have driven four hundred yards, never mind four hundred miles. Anyway, I was with Jackie.'

'The original case against you suggested your wife was leaving you and you were trying to stop her,' said Norman.

'Yeah, and I told them it was bollocks in court, and I'm telling you the same now. If she were going to leave, she would have told me. In fact, if she had wanted to split from me she wouldn't have left — she would have kicked me out. I would have come home one day and found all my clothes outside and the locks changed.'

'The police suggested your wife was scared of you,' said Slater.

Harris laughed. 'Yeah, right. That was a load of cobblers too. My wife wasn't scared of anyone.'

'She wasn't scared of you?'

'Why would she be?'

'You're a big, strong guy,' said Slater, 'and we've just seen you've got a bit of a temper. I understand you've had one or two scraps since you've been in here.'

Harris gave Slater a pitying look. 'Of course, I've got a bloody temper. If you had been locked up in here for ten years for something you didn't do, I don't think you'd be too happy, would you? And, for your information, I've never started a fight in here. When you're a big guy like me, you become a target for anyone who's trying to make a name for themselves as a hard man.'

Slater knew this was true enough. 'So, you're telling us you were a pussycat where your wife was concerned?'

'Look, I'd never been in a fight in my life until I got locked in here,' said Harris. 'Violence is not my thing, and it never was. Believe it or not, I loved my wife more than anything, and I would never have raised a finger to her.'

'Why was she leaving you?' asked Norman.

'I already told you, she wasn't leaving me.'

'But she had a bag packed,' said Slater. 'She had it with her when she was found.'

'Yes, I know,' said Harris. 'I was asked to identify it. But if she was leaving, don't you think she would have packed a bit more stuff? What she had was an overnight bag.'

'If the bag didn't mean she was leaving, what was it for?' asked Norman.

Harris shifted uncomfortably. 'What do you think it was for?'

'You think she was planning to spend a dirty weekend with someone else?' asked Slater. 'Only that would be enough motive for some men to—'

'There you go again, assuming I'm guilty,' said Harris.

'I'm just saying jealousy is more than enough motive for a lot of husbands. Are you telling me you weren't jealous?'

'Sure, I was jealous, but I cheated on her often enough. I could hardly blame her for wanting to get her own back, could I?'

'I'm finding it difficult to get my head around your relationship with your wife,' said Slater. 'You say you loved her, yet now you're admitting you were cheating on her. Sleeping around was what for you? A hobby?'

'Look, I like women and women like me. I can't help it. It's just how it is. My wife knew that. She didn't like it much, but she accepted it, most of the time.'

'And what about those times she didn't accept it?' asked Norman. 'According to the information we have, you and your wife argued on a regular basis.'

'Argued and fought,' said Harris. 'Yes, I can't disagree with that. Whenever she suspected I'd been up to something, she'd create merry hell and make me pay for it.'

'And that's when you'd give her a good slap, right?' asked Slater.

'No, you're wrong. I never laid a finger on her. She was the one who did the punching and slapping.'

'Oh, come on. She was barely five feet tall, and you expect us to believe she was beating you up?'

Harris stared back at Slater. 'I realise you don't get it, but we were different from most couples, right? You can't condemn me just because you don't see how a relationship like that could work.'

Slater didn't understand how a relationship could be sustainable in a state of almost constant conflict, but he felt there was nothing to be gained by riling Harris any more than he already had.

'I promise you she wasn't averse to hitting me with any weapon that was handy,' said Harris. 'She even came at me with a kitchen knife once.'

'What did you do to deserve that?' asked Norman.

'We'd been at a party. Julie caught me flirting with her sister. She didn't say anything to me at the time, but when we got home, she went crazy. I swear if I'd had my back turned she would have buried that knife right up to the hilt.'

'You make Julie sound like a psychopath,' said Slater. 'No one else mentions ever seeing these violent tendencies.'

Harris gave a sad, but fond, little smile. 'No one else lived with her and cheated on her, did they?'

'So why were you flirting with her sister?' asked Norman.

'It's just what I do, right? If I was a Hollywood celebrity, I could claim I was addicted to sex, and everyone would feel sorry for me as I went into rehab, but because I'm just some ordinary bloke I'm not allowed to use that as a reason.'

'That's not a reason,' said Slater. 'It's a lame excuse used by people who get caught.'

Harris glared at Slater.

'Let's go back to the weekend when Julie died,' said Norman, hastily. 'You said she was planning to spend the weekend with another man? What makes you so sure?'

'I wasn't sure at first,' said Harris, finally tearing his eyes away from Slater. 'She told me she was going to stay with an old friend, and I believed her. It was when they found her in that caravan with the bag that I realised what she must have been planning.'

'What about the friend?' asked Slater.

'That was the thing. There never was one. It turns Julie was as good a liar as I was.'

'And you never suspected?' asked Norman.

Harris smiled ruefully. 'I trusted her. It's ironic, isn't it?'

'She left here on Friday afternoon, but you didn't report her missing until mid-morning on Monday. Why was that?'

'Because her sister Jackie was with me until Monday morning. I could hardly report my wife missing while her sister was there, could I?'

'Jackie was still there?' asked Slater. 'That wasn't perfect planning, was it? Unless, of course, you knew Julie wasn't going to be coming back.'

Harris glared at Slater again. 'Are you sure you're here to help me? Only you seem to be making everything I say into another reason to convict me.'

'I'm here to find out what happened, and to point out all the glaring holes in your story — just like the prosecution will if you appeal.'

'You might not like it, Steve, but Dave's right,' said Norman. 'If you were expecting Julie back on Sunday night, why was Jackie still there?'

'Because I couldn't get her to leave. She didn't want to go back home. It was probably my fault. We'd talked about me leaving Julie to be with her.'

'This would be the Julie you love so much, right?' asked Slater, his voice thick with sarcasm.

'Yes, I loved her, but I also made her unhappy on a regular basis.'

'And you think leaving her to live with her sister would have made her happy?'

'I used to think it would probably be better for her if I were out of her life.'

'And getting together with Jackie was suddenly going to change your sex addict ways, was it?' asked Slater.

'No, of course not. I probably would have made Jackie unhappy too.'

'Let's get back to Jackie,' said Norman. 'Why didn't she want to go home?'

'Because she was terrified of her husband.' He looked pointedly at Slater. 'Now there was a bloke who did like to knock his wife around.'

'In that case, I should think her going missing for a weekend would have given him a good excuse to beat the crap out of her,' replied Slater.

'He didn't know,' said Harris. 'He was away that weekend.'

'I thought Jackie told everyone she was at home with him all weekend,' said Norman.

Harris sighed. 'There's no way she would have spent the weekend with me if he had been at home. He's a control freak. He wouldn't let her out for five minutes on her own, never mind for a whole weekend.'

'Where was he?'

'Probably with his mates at a football match.'

'Until Monday afternoon?' asked Slater.

'He supports Newcastle United. Him and his mates have season tickets. They would often leave on Friday morning and be away until Monday afternoon. It was just an excuse for a three- or four-day bender while his terrified wife was sitting at home waiting for him to come home and beat the shit out her.'

'Why wasn't this brought up at the trial?'

'Because Jackie backed him up and insisted they were both at home all weekend. The police said that was good enough and didn't bother to check it out because they had already made their minds up I was guilty.'

'But you could have insisted—'

'Look,' said Harris, 'I saw what he did to her when the police told him I was suggesting she was my alibi. Imagine what he would have done if I had insisted and she had been forced to admit she was with me? He would probably have killed her.'

'You're saying you've done ten years inside, so your sister-in-law wouldn't get beaten up?'

'The woman I loved had been murdered,' said Harris. 'I couldn't let that happen to her sister too.'

There was a brief silence as they considered this.

'Does he still have a Newcastle season ticket?' asked Slater.

Harris gave him a grim look. 'How the hell would I know? He's not exactly a regular visitor.'

'Yeah, of course, sorry,' Slater said, chastened. 'That was a stupid question.'

'You say Eddie Smith used to go to football with his mates,' said Norman. 'Can you recall any names?'

'I remember the James brothers,' said Harris. 'Billy and Ken. They're a pair of hard cases, a perfect match for Smith — three thugs together.'

* * *

'It's good to see you have the bit between your teeth,' said Norman, as they drove away from the prison, 'but don't forget — we're supposed to be proving this guy's innocent. You were pretty hard on him back there.'

'Yeah, I suppose I was a bit,' admitted Slater. 'I want to make sure he's not taking us for a ride, that's all.'

'And what have you decided? Are we being conned?'

'There are a lot of holes in this case on both sides, so I'm keeping an open mind for now.'

'What about this Eddie Smith?' asked Norman.

'Yeah, he sounds like a regular Mr Nice Guy, doesn't he? Just the sort of man every father dreads their daughter ever getting involved with.'

'He has to be a suspect. If he knew his wife was involved with Harris, maybe he killed Julie and framed Harris as revenge.'

'Maybe,' said Slater, 'but if what Harris said about him is right, Smith is the sort of guy who would be more likely to kill his own wife — especially if he had so much as an inkling she was even thinking about another guy.'

'Even so, I think we should add him to the list of suspects,' said Norman.

'Oh, for sure. The man's a thug. We certainly can't rule him out.'

CHAPTER EIGHT

It was after three p.m. by the time they pulled into the car park outside the office. As soon as Norman switched off the engine, Slater swung his door open, but then stopped without climbing out.

'Are you expecting visitors?' he asked Norman.

'What?'

'Two people are waiting in a car outside your office, and they know who we are.'

'Hey, don't let them get away.' Norman tried to squint past Slater to see who the visitors were. 'If they're clients, we can't afford to lose them.'

Slater watched the man and woman as they climbed from the car. The man was in his mid to late twenties, and everything about him said plainclothes police officer. He might as well have been wearing a sign. Slater guessed the woman was in her late thirties, or possibly early forties. Her hair was cut short, and she wore a smart suit. There was an air of calm authority about her that indicated she was the younger man's boss. They both looked as though they hadn't had much sleep.

'I don't think these two are clients,' said Slater. 'Not unless the local constabulary are going to ask us to start solving crimes for them.'

As he climbed from the car, Slater did his best to ignore the couple, but they were focusing on him. As he waited for Norman to unlock the office door, the man called out. 'David Slater?'

Norman had the door half open, but now he stopped and turned to the couple. Slater looked the man up and down. 'Who's asking?'

The man held up a warrant card. 'DS Wesley.' He indicted his female companion. 'And this is DI Robbins. We'd like to ask you a few questions.'

'What about?'

'Can we come inside?' asked Robbins. 'It's a bit cold out here.'

Norman pushed the door open and led the way inside, Robbins following behind. Slater stepped back to let Wesley in, but the younger man waved him inside first.

'Can I ask what this is about?' asked Slater once they were inside.

Wesley opened a folder and handed Slater a photograph. 'Do you recognise this number plate?'

'Yes, it's my car registration number. Why are you showing me this?'

'Do you know where your car is, Mr Slater?'

'Look, what is this? Has there been an accident or something?'

Robbins took over now. 'Are we to assume you don't know where your car is?'

'Not exactly,' said Slater. 'I lent it to a friend. Look, what's going on? Has there been an accident? Is she alright?'

Robbins' eyebrows raised momentarily, but Wesley's surprise was much more noticeable. 'Your friend is a woman?' he asked.

'Yes, she's a woman. What's wrong with that?'

'There's nothing wrong with it, it's just not what we were expecting.'

'Now you're starting to worry me,' said Slater. 'Unless procedures have changed a lot in the past month or so, car crime doesn't get investigated by a DI and a DS, so can you please tell me what's going on?'

Robbins nodded to Wesley, who slipped another photograph from his folder. 'This photograph was taken shortly after midnight. The car had just been parked in a public car park when this happened.'

Slater looked at the crumpled wreck in the photograph in disbelief. The car was the right model, the right colour, and the registration number was undoubtedly his. Norman hurried over and peered over his shoulder. 'Jeez! It looks like it was hit by a missile!'

'What happened to the driver?' asked Slater. 'Is she alright?'

'There was no trace of a woman anywhere near the car, Mr Slater.'

'Are you sure?'

Robbins nodded to Wesley again, and he produced yet another photograph. 'We think this man was driving the car,' said Robbins. 'As it was your car, the first responders thought he was you, but we soon realised that wasn't the case. We were rather hoping you might be able to tell us who he is.'

Slater stared at the obviously dead face and shook his head. 'Sorry, I have no idea. Who is he?'

'We don't know yet. He had no ID on him, not even a phone, that's why we were hoping you could tell us.'

Slater passed the photo on to Norman. 'Do you know this bloke, Norm?'

Norman took the photo and stared at it. 'I have no idea who he is,' he said, handing the photo back to Wesley, 'but he looks pretty dead.'

Wesley ignored Norman and focused his attention on Slater. 'You're quite sure you don't know him?'

'I repeat — I do not know him,' said Slater, patiently.

Norman had been studying the photograph of Slater's car, and now he voiced his thoughts. 'You say this car was in a car park, right? So, this damage isn't the result of another car crashing into it, is it? If I had to guess, I'd have to say this was bomb damage.'

Robbins gave Norman an appreciative look. 'I'd have to say you were correct.'

'I was a DS in London,' explained Norman. 'I've come across one or two of these before.'

Slater was still struggling to take it all in. 'A bomb? That's a bit random, isn't it?'

'Well, that's the thing,' said Robbins. 'Who goes around randomly bombing cars parked in out-of-the-way car parks in Winchester? If you wanted to cause a bit of mayhem, you'd choose a busy car park when there were likely to be lots of people around. But, of course, if you were looking to murder a specific person, planting a bomb under their car has been known to work before.'

'What? You mean me?' asked Slater. 'Why would anyone want to blow me up?'

Robbins inclined her head thoughtfully. 'Let's get back to your car. You say you lent it to your girlfriend . . . could she have lent it to this man?'

'No way,' said Slater. 'She wouldn't do that. I know she wouldn't.'

'Okay, so is it possible this man could have stolen it from wherever she had parked it?'

'I find that hard to believe.'

Robbins sighed. 'Look, I understand it must be a bit of a shock to find your car has been reduced to scrap metal, but the fact remains that a man is dead, presumably killed by a bomb that someone planted under your car. You're a detective, you know we need answers, but at the moment you're not providing any, are you?'

Slater could see the sincerity on Robbins' face, and he knew she was right. 'I came back from Thailand on Monday evening. The girl I was with had to get back to London because she was starting a new job the next morning, so I lent her my car. She said she would keep it safely parked until she had a chance to bring it back down here.'

'Parked where?'

'I'm not sure.'

'You lent your girlfriend a fifty-grand car, and you don't even know where it is?' asked Wesley, doubtfully.

'She's not my girlfriend,' said Slater, testily. 'She's just a friend who happens to be a police officer who works up in London. I'm happy to lend her my car because I know she's done almost every type of advanced driver training there is. She was taking it straight to her new job, where there is a secure car park, and she wasn't going to use it again until she brought it back here.'

'Where is this secure car park?'

'I don't know its exact location, just somewhere in London.'

'It doesn't look as if it was very safe or secure to me,' said Wesley, nodding at the photograph. 'What was it doing in Winchester if it was supposed to be in London?'

'I don't know!' Slater could see Wesley didn't believe a word he was saying. 'Look, I'd phone her, but she sent me a text yesterday saying she wouldn't be able to bring my car back for a few days because she was going to be unavailable.'

'Unavailable?' What does that mean?' asked Robbins.

'I don't know. She just started a new job, so maybe she's on an induction course.'

'Didn't you ask?' asked Wesley.

'Why would I?'

'If I were you, I'd want to know when my car was coming back.'

'But you're not me, are you?'

'This all sounds a bit iffy if you ask me,' said Wesley.

Slater bristled. 'Iffy? What d'you mean, iffy?'

'Alright, Mr Slater, let's calm down, shall we?' said Robbins. 'I think what my colleague is trying to say is that it's all a bit vague. I'm sure when you think about what you've told us so far, you'll agree with him.'

Norman put a calming hand on Slater's shoulder. 'Come on, Dave, take it easy. I don't think DS Wesley meant it like that, and they do have a point. I know you're not trying to be awkward, but you have to admit, you're not helping much, are you?'

Slater heaved a big sigh and wished he knew what the hell was going on. 'I understand where you're coming from, but I can't tell you anything, because I don't know anything,' he told Robbins.

'You could tell me who your friend is,' she said. 'Maybe she can explain how your car came to be in Winchester.'

Slater reached for a pen and a notepad. 'I'll write it down for you,' he said, adding pointedly, 'but I'd prefer it if you could check her out personally, and be discreet, will you?'

Robbins raised one eyebrow.

'No, she's not married, but as I said, she's a police officer too. I'm not exactly a police service pinup boy at the moment, and it might not do her prospects any good if her bosses became aware she spent two weeks in Thailand with me.'

Small crinkly lines appeared briefly around Robbins' eyes, accompanying the tiny smile that betrayed her amusement. 'I'll see what I can do.'

Slater finished writing and handed the paper to Robbins. 'What about my car?'

'You know how it works. It's part of an investigation, and right now I'm not sure if you're a central part of that investigation or not. For now, I think I'd prefer it if you let us do our jobs and wait until you hear from us.'

Slater watched helplessly as Robbins and Wesley left. 'Did that really happen?' he asked.

'I'm afraid it did,' said Norman. 'Are you okay?'

'Well, yeah, I suppose so.'

'You're not going to start charging all over the place trying to find out who did this, are you?'

'I'll decide on that after I've spoken to Watson and she's explained how my car has come to be in a thousand pieces in a Winchester car park!'

CHAPTER NINE

Slater listened as the ringtone went on and on, finally going to voicemail. He had been calling Watson throughout the day since Robbins and Wesley had left, and he must have called well over a dozen times now, but still there was no answer. In the beginning, he thought maybe she had been hurt last night, but he was coming to the conclusion she was avoiding him, although he had no idea why. Perhaps this time he should leave a message.

'Hi, Sam, it's me,' he said after the beep. 'I've got a bit of a problem. The police have been on to me about my car being blown up in Winchester last night. I had to tell them you borrowed it, but they want proof, so I've given them your number. DI Robbins will be contacting you, but I'd like to speak to you first, please. I need to know what's going on and if you're alright. Give me a call when you get this message.'

He ended the call, dropped into an armchair, tossed the phone down, and closed his eyes. Not surprisingly, he couldn't stop thinking about what had happened earlier, and now his head was throbbing. He tried to switch his thoughts away from his problems, but it was easier said than done. And then his phone started to ring.

He snatched it up and looked at the caller ID. He didn't recognise the number, but something made him put the phone to his ear anyway.

'Is that you, Dave?'

'Sam?'

'Hi.'

'Are you alright?'

'I'm fine, but I thought we agreed we weren't going to do this.'

'I'm sorry, I wouldn't have called, but this is important. Did you get my message?'

'Yes, I got your message, but I wish you had asked me before you gave my details out to all and sundry.'

'All and sundry? I gave your number to one DI, and she promised to be discreet. You know I wouldn't have done that if I hadn't been desperate.'

'What do you mean desperate?'

'I said in the message. My bloody car has been blown up in a car park in Winchester. You're supposed to be looking after it, so I was worried what had happened to you and wondering what the hell my car was doing there?'

'Don't be so ridiculous! Your car is safely parked where I said it would be.'

'But I've seen the photographs. I know it's my car, it's got my bloody licence plates. Apparently, some unidentified bloke was driving the car, but someone had planted a bomb under it. It detonated in the car park and blew this guy up. The police reckon I was the target.'

'That's absurd. I told you, your car's safe and sound exactly where I left it.'

'Okay, in that case, I need you to confirm you have the car and where you were last night. That's the only reason I gave DI Robbins your number.'

'But I was out last night.'

'What, in my car?'

'No, of course not. I told you, your car is right where I said it would be, and it hasn't been blown up.'

'But it must have been. I told you, I've seen the photos.'

'And I've seen your car,' said Watson, irritably. 'It was in the car park when I came in this morning.'

'Could someone have taken it?'

'You're not listening to me,' cried Watson. 'Your car is parked in a very secure police car park, that's guarded twenty-four seven. I had to have special permission to park it there, and the only person who is authorised to remove it is me.'

'Where is this car park?'

'I can't tell you that.'

'What d'you mean you can't tell me?'

'We agreed you wouldn't ask me about my new job.'

'I'm not asking about your job; I'm asking about my car. I've got the police showing me a photograph of a bomb wreck, and you're telling me they've got it all wrong. Come on, Sam, help me out here!'

'I promise you I'll talk to DI Robbins and tell her where your car is, but you can't keep contacting me. We agreed.'

Slater couldn't quite believe what he was hearing. What was the matter with the woman? Why couldn't she understand his predicament? 'I don't keep contacting you. It's one phone call, and it's an emergency. I thought we were still friends.'

'We are still friends, but we agreed we weren't in a relationship and we weren't going to try and turn it into one.'

'I don't know what's wrong with you,' said Slater, exasperated. 'I'm not trying to turn anything into a relationship. I'm just asking you to speak to the police. That's reasonable enough in the circumstances, isn't it? I thought friends helped each other out.'

'I will help you out, I promise, but I have to go now.'

There was a loud click and the call ended. Slater looked at the phone in disbelief and put it to his ear again, but she had gone.

As he was looking in disgust at his phone, Norman came into the room. 'You look like you lost a fifty-pound note and found a fiver,' he said.

'That was Sam. She's pissed off at me for giving Robbins her number. She's just hung up on me.'

'Maybe it's just me, but it doesn't seem unreasonable to ask a friend to prove where your car was when they had your car and it's now a wreck.'

'Apparently we're not that sort of friend.'

'I thought you two parted on good terms. Mature adults. Wasn't that the phrase you used?'

Slater reached for his phone again. 'You're right, Norm. It's not unreasonable to ask where my car is. I'm going to call her again, only this time I'm going to get some real answers.'

'Well, good luck with that,' said Norman. 'I'm going out, and I don't know what time I'll be back, so don't wait up.'

CHAPTER TEN

When Norman arrived back at Slater's at 7.30 the next morning, he could see his friend had obviously not slept well. He was eating his breakfast and trying, unsuccessfully, to look cheerful. 'What's the story with you and Watson?'

'There is no me and Watson.'

'I meant what's her story about the car?'

'I have no idea. She won't return any of my calls. That's why I say there is no me and Watson.'

'You're finished?'

'I guess that's what it means.'

'But this isn't the action of two grown-ups, is it? I may not know Watson as you do, but I can't believe she would finish with you in this way. I'm sure she would tell you to your face.'

Slater shrugged. 'You'd think so, wouldn't you, but the evidence seems to suggest you're wrong.'

'Maybe something happened to her,' said Norman.

'Something has happened to my bloody car, but I can't get any sense out of her.'

'Did you do something to piss her off?'

'All I did was ask about my car? If anyone has a right to be pissed off, it's me, not her!'

Norman wasn't convinced, and he stared hard at Slater. 'You knew this was going to happen, didn't you?'

'What? You think I knew she was going to have my car destroyed?'

'You know that's not what I meant. Why wouldn't she want to speak to you, or to see you?'

'Maybe she realised how boring I am,' said Slater, but he kept his eyes averted.

'No, I don't buy that,' said Norman. 'She can't have thought you were boring or she would never have agreed to spend ten nights in Thailand with you. Anyway, I thought you told me she liked the new, adult Dave Slater even better than the old one.'

'Sometimes things just aren't meant to be,' said Slater. 'And the new, adult me is prepared to accept that without the need to make a big deal out of it.'

Norman studied Slater as he tried to work out what was what. 'You told her it was over, didn't you? But you haven't seen her, so when did you do that?'

Slater shrugged again.

'Oh, no. Don't tell me you did it by text! Jesus, how adult is that?'

'I did not end it by text,' said Slater. 'If you must know, when we got off the plane from Thailand I told her we should give each other some space for a while.'

'What? Why would you do that? What possible reason could you have?'

'She misled me.'

'What do you mean she misled you?'

'She told me something the day before we left Thailand that she should have told me sooner.'

'What did she tell you?'

'That she has a daughter.'

Norman hadn't been expecting that and was momentarily lost for words, but he quickly recovered. 'So? What's the problem? Jane has three kids. It didn't put me off.'

'But you knew about them before you became an item.'

'Well, yeah, that's true, but did you consider how she might have wanted to tell you but found it difficult? I could imagine there are a whole lot of guys who'd like to spend a few nights with Watson but would run a mile if she mentioned a kid afterwards.'

Slater looked distinctly uncomfortable.

'Touch a nerve there, did I?' asked Norman. 'That's what you did, isn't it? You didn't mind sharing a bed with her, but then as soon as she mentioned a kid you dropped her like a hot potato!'

'That's not fair,' began Slater.

'You're right — it's not fair. It's not fair to Watson. Did you give her a chance to explain?'

'I told you, I've been deceived before. If she had told me the truth from the start—'

'Oh, come on, Dave, not that again! It was twenty years ago, and Debbie was cheating on you! It's not the same thing at all. Are you going to let that ruin the rest of your life? So, Watson has a kid. It's not the end of the world. Kids are great. They keep you young. Has it occurred to you that you might like having one around?'

Slater stared miserably down at his feet. 'I'm not sure I'd know where to start.'

'Do you think anyone does? Jeez, even people who plan to have kids have no idea where to start when they arrive. Do you think I knew what to do when I first met Jane's kids? I was over fifty, and I had to face three of them!'

'Yeah, but I've always been awkward with kids. You're different. You're much more outgoing than me.'

'D'you think you're the only introvert in the world? There are plenty of people out there just like you who have kids and love them.'

'But I'd been working with her for months, and she never once mentioned it. We used to stay away from home all week. How could she do that?'

'Maybe she thought you'd regard her as somehow less able to focus on her work if you knew.'

'But how could she stay away from her daughter all week?'

'Says the guy who hasn't seen, or spoken to, his mother in months.'

'That's different, and you know it.'

Norman wasn't going to argue that one; instead, he jumped to Watson's defence. 'If the job were her only way of providing for the child, she would have to do whatever it takes. It doesn't mean she wanted to be away from home. She must have had a good support network to help with the childcare, but you won't know because you haven't given her a chance to explain, have you?'

Slater shrugged unhappily but offered no defence, so Norman carried on. 'I don't see how you can criticise if you haven't asked her for her side of the story.'

'I suppose if you put it like that—'

'How come you didn't find out when you went to her place after you quit your job? Kids have loads of stuff. It's usually everywhere.'

Slater hadn't thought about this, and Norman could see a spark of curiosity.

'Now you come to mention it, there was no kid's stuff anywhere. It was just a small flat.'

'It sounds to me like you need to ask some questions,' said Norman.

'I can't believe I didn't think of that when she told me.'

'Maybe there was a custody battle, and the girl is with her father and her mum doesn't have much access. Or maybe deep inside you were waiting to play your "get out of jail free card" and jumped at the opportunity without thinking.'

A retort was on the tip of Slater's tongue, but he managed to hold on to it. 'Yeah, well, it's done now,' he said, miserably.

'So, undo it.'

'It's not that simple.'

'Yes, it is,' said Norman. 'You told her you needed some space, right?'

Slater said nothing.

'That is what you told her, isn't it?' insisted Norman.

'Yes.'

'Well then, now you've had some space, you can use the return of your car as an excuse to get in touch and tell her you'd like to see her again and hear her side of the story.'

'I dunno . . .'

'I'm sorry,' said Norman, 'but I could have sworn you told me you liked her.'

'Well, yeah, I do.'

'So how about you start behaving like the new, adult Dave Slater you claim to be, and do something about it. The only way you're ever going to get past this "deceit" thing is if you face up to it instead of hiding behind it. It's like you think you deserve some pure, angel-like woman who's perfect in every way, is that it?'

Slater was studying his feet and wouldn't look up, so Norman continued his lecture. 'You need to get it into your head that this fantasy woman you're waiting for doesn't exist, and why should she? None of us are perfect, so what right do we have to expect anyone else to be? Unless, of course, you somehow think you're better than the rest of us?'

'Of course, I don't.'

'Well, then, Mr Adult, you need to accept Wonder Woman doesn't exist and get real, because if you keep on looking for her, you're just going to end up a sad and lonely old man.'

Slater looked up, red-eyed. 'You think so?'

'I might be wrong, but I can't believe Watson had any intention of deceiving you. My guess is she was too professional to mention it at first, and then maybe she just found it more difficult as time went on. Maybe she's in a complicated situation and she doesn't know how to handle it. If you ask her, maybe you'll find out.'

'You make it sound easy.'

'That's because it is,' said Norman. 'The only thing that's stopping you is you. You've got nothing to lose, because if you let this deceit thing win now, you've lost her for good anyway. If it were me, I'd give her a chance.'

Slater said nothing and went back to contemplating his shoes. Norman stepped forward and patted his shoulder. 'Look, I'm sorry. I just thought it needed to be said. I think you're a great guy, and I don't want to see you turn into some bitter, lonely, old man.'

'It's okay,' said Slater. 'I appreciate your honesty, even if I don't necessarily agree with it.'

'You don't care about your car, do you?'

'At the end of the day, it's just a car. I would like to know what the hell's going on, though. A guy died, and it might be because of me.'

'But even that's not what's worrying you, is it?'

Slater let out a long heavy sigh. 'It's Sam,' he said. 'I don't understand how she's involved in this, but I'm sure she is somehow.'

'Do we need to put our case on hold?'

'That wouldn't be right, would it? We took on the job, so we need to get on with it. Besides, Robbins looked as if she knew what she was doing, and she won't appreciate us getting under her feet. Let's see what she can dig up first.'

'Right,' agreed Norman.

There was an uneasy silence for the first few minutes of their journey to work that morning, but Slater and Norman had disagreed before. They both knew any bad blood between them would soon be gone, and by the time they reached their office things were back to normal.

CHAPTER ELEVEN

They had been inside the office less than five minutes when there was a knock on the door, and it swung open. It was DI Robbins and DS Wesley. Robbins smiled, but Wesley could only manage a scowl.

Norman looked up from his tea-making. 'I guess that's two more teas, then, right?'

'Oh, yes please,' said Robbins. 'I could murder a cup of tea.'

'Back already?' asked Slater. 'I didn't expect to see you so soon. Didn't Sam Brearley put you straight about the car?'

'Ah, yes, your mysterious friend DS Samantha Brearley, also known as Watson because she's so good with H.O.L.M.E.S.' Robbins' voice was heavy with sarcasm.

'What?' asked Slater.

Robbins sighed. 'I'm afraid your friend is proving rather hard to find.'

'What do you mean? I gave you her contact details yesterday.'

'Have you tried contacting her since we spoke, Mr Slater?'

'Well, yeah, I wanted to know what had happened to my car.'

'And did she answer her phone?'

Slater's instincts told him he should tread carefully here. 'No, she didn't answer her phone.'

'Now there's a coincidence,' said Robbins. 'I left several messages yesterday, but when I got no response, I tried tracking her down using other methods. Now I'm beginning to wonder if DS Samantha Brearley actually exists.'

'Don't talk bollocks,' said Slater. 'She was my DS! We worked together for a few months. She had a warrant card and everything. She flew out to join me in Thailand. I saw her passport when we checked in on the way back.'

Slater couldn't read Robbins' face, but it was clear what Wesley thought. He looked at Robbins again, and she shrugged as she spoke. 'All I can tell you is that she didn't show up when I tried searching the police database yesterday.'

'That doesn't make sense.'

'You said she was starting a new job. Did she tell you what that job was?'

'No, she didn't. She liked to keep work separate from her private life.'

'Do you know her home address?'

'No, I never had any need to know it.'

Now Robbins stared at him, and Slater knew she — rightly — didn't believe him.

'Really? You expect me to believe you spent months working with this woman, even going on holiday together, and you have no idea where she lives.'

'We worked away. We stayed in hotels during the week and went our separate ways on weekends. I didn't need to know where she lived.'

Robbins stared at Slater. He knew she was weighing him up, and he wondered how close he was to being taken back to Winchester for questioning.

'DS Wesley would like to ask you a few more questions about the man who died when your car blew up.'

'What questions?'

Wesley opened the folder he was carrying and handed Slater a photograph. 'Do you still claim you don't know this man, Mr Slater?'

Slater looked at the photograph. 'I told you I didn't know him yesterday, and I still don't know him today.'

'You're quite sure about that?'

'Yes, I'm sure. Who is he?'

'We'll come to that,' said Wesley, slipping another photo from the file. 'How about this one?'

Slater did a double take and looked at Wesley. 'Are you trying to be funny?'

'Do I look as though I'm laughing?'

'This is me,' said Slater, 'unless I've got a double somewhere. Where did you get it?'

'It was on the dead man's phone, along with your home address.'

'I thought you said you didn't have his phone.'

'It was in his rucksack,' said Wesley. 'It got blown across the car park and didn't get found until late yesterday afternoon. Why do you think he had your photograph?'

'I have no idea,' said Slater. 'Perhaps he was looking for a pair of detectives to solve a case.'

The sarcasm flew, unnoticed, over Wesley's head. 'There are no photos of Mr Norman anywhere and no mention of his name,' he said. 'He only seems to have been interested in you. I'm still waiting for you to tell me why.'

Slater sighed. He had come across in-your-face young coppers like Wesley many times before. 'Well, I'm afraid you're going to have a long wait. I can't tell you what I don't know.' He tapped the photo. 'And this bloke can't tell you because he's dead. Perhaps we'd get a bit further if you tell me who he is and why you think I should know him.'

Robbins had been studying Slater's face. 'We might have drawn a blank with your girlfriend' — she clearly knew that would annoy Slater — 'but things have been moving quite fast with the investigation into what actually happened to your car. When we found bits of that man scattered around your car, we thought he'd been blown up by a bomb that had been planted under the car earlier.

'Now we know who he is, we believe he was actually attaching the bomb to your car while it was in the car park, but somehow managed to detonate it while he was still there. At the moment, we're thinking he had just placed it under the car and for some reason it went off as he stood up. His face was undamaged because he must have been turning away as it went off. Everything from the waist down was mincemeat.'

'You know who he is, then?' asked Slater.

'His name is, or was, Yuri Lenkov.'

Slater stiffened. 'Lenkov? What's that, Russian?'

'That's where he originates from, but more recently he's based himself in London, working for whoever wants to hire him. He's believed to have carried out at least two murders using car bombs, and as he was carrying your photograph, we have to consider the distinct possibility he may have been down here looking to complete his hat trick.'

'But why would he want to kill me?'

'That's what we were hoping you could tell us. He's never been known to work outside London before, and yet, just a day after you arrive back from Thailand, here he is in Winchester with your photo and your address, planting a bomb under your car. It's a bit of a coincidence, don't you think?'

'You're saying he's a hitman?' asked Norman. 'I worked up in London for years, and I don't recall ever seeing that face or hearing that name.'

'My colleagues in London tell me he's a recent addition,' said Robbins. 'He only came to anyone's attention in the last couple of years, so he wouldn't have been around when you were still working there.'

'You've done your homework, then,' said Slater.

'You've been a DI. You know it always pays to know as much as you can before you start asking questions. Or are you still a DI? I couldn't quite make out exactly what your status is.'

'Definitely an ex-DI,' said Slater. 'I won't bore you with the details.'

Robbins was waiting for more, but Slater wasn't forthcoming, so she dug a little deeper. 'Like you said, I've done my homework, so I know this wouldn't be the first time a Russian has crossed your path.'

Slater had been expecting this to come up as soon as he heard the Russian-sounding name. 'If you're referring to the guy who waved a gun in my face, that was ages ago now, and I can assure you I can recall his face in great detail. It's not the same guy.'

'That must have been a pretty unnerving experience,' said Wesley.

Slater gave the young DS a withering look. 'You think? Let me tell you, looking down the barrel of a gun held by a hardened killer scared the shit out of me, and I'm not ashamed to admit it. I certainly wouldn't recommend it.'

'He didn't shoot you though, did he?'

'What's that supposed to mean?'

'Well, there must have been some reason why he let you go.'

The inference was clear, but Robbins apparently hadn't been expecting Wesley to start drawing his own conclusions just yet. 'That's enough, Jason,' she said. 'I don't think there's any doubt about what happened back then, and I'm not aware of any reason we should question it.'

The young DS looked suitably chastened, but Slater wasn't going to let it lie there. 'I don't know what you're trying to imply, Sergeant,' he said, looking daggers at Wesley, 'but if you read the case notes, you'll see the conclusion the senior officers came to is that he never intended to shoot me. The whole episode was designed to scare the crap out of me, and I can assure you it did, almost literally.'

Wesley grinned at Slater. He might have annoyed Robbins, but he had been hoping to get under Slater's skin, and now it seemed he had succeeded. 'And you're quite sure you've never met this man?' he asked, again.

'How many more times do I have to deny it?'

Wesley smiled a wicked smile. 'In that case, Mr Slater,' he said, slowly withdrawing yet another photograph from the folder, 'how do you explain this?'

The photograph showed Slater and Watson sitting at a table in an airport lounge. They were looking up at the dead man, who appeared to be speaking to Slater.

Slater's mouth had dropped open. He studied the photograph for a minute before he spoke. 'Where did you get this?'

'Again, it was on his phone. It looks to me like you were having a conversation with this recently murdered man you claim never to have set eyes on.'

'Now don't get ahead of yourself. I said I didn't know him. It's not the same thing.'

'But you have to admit that it does look as if you're speaking to him.'

'That doesn't mean I know him, does it? I could be saying "no, that seat's not taken",' said Slater. 'The fact we appear to be speaking proves nothing. If you wanted to ask someone if there was an empty seat at their table, would you introduce yourself first?'

'I suppose not,' said Wesley, reluctantly.

'It's obviously not a selfie unless he's got another pair of arms ten feet long, so he must have given someone else his phone and asked them to take the picture.'

'Why would he do that?'

'I don't know,' said Slater. 'Perhaps it's so you could come and ask me a load of stupid questions. Or maybe he wants to frame me.' He had been hoping to get a reaction from Wesley, but the younger man didn't oblige.

'Frame you for what?'

Slater sighed his exasperation. 'I appreciate you're quite new to this, but surely even you can understand that the basic idea behind framing someone is that they don't know anything about it until it's too late.'

'Of course, I know that,' said Wesley.

'So why do you expect me to know the answer?' asked Slater, through gritted teeth.

'Alright then. Can you tell us how you and Mr Lenkov appear to be speaking to each other in this photograph?'

'No, I can't, unless it's like I said, and he asked about a seat,' admitted Slater. 'I can tell you one thing, though. That photograph must have been taken an hour or so before I boarded my flight home from Thailand, yet you say your man rarely leaves London. Has it occurred to you it could have been manipulated?'

Wesley tried to look sceptical, but instead, he looked guilty. 'Manipulated? How d'you mean?'

'Photoshopped, of course. How d'you think I mean?'

The young detective's face told its own story.

'You haven't even considered the possibility, have you?' asked Slater. 'I suggest you get it checked out to make sure it's genuine before you jump to conclusions about my relationship with the guy.'

Robbins could see Wesley was about to be swallowed up by the hole he was digging for himself. 'We'll get it checked,' she said, hastily. 'Are you sure the photo couldn't have been taken at any other time?'

'No chance,' said Slater. 'It's the only time I've ever waited in an airport lounge with the girl in the photograph.'

'Is that who I think it is?'

'Yes, this is DS Samantha Brearley, the friend who borrowed my car,' said Slater. 'At least now you can see she does exist.'

Robbins smiled. 'I can see someone was with you in the airport lounge, but it doesn't prove who she is, does it?'

'But what would be the point in me lying?' said Slater. Then he had an idea. 'You can check the flight log. That will tell you what name she was using, won't it?'

'Can you remember your seat number?' asked Wesley, who was writing this down.

'No, but we were by the centre emergency exits where there's extra legroom. She was sitting in the window seat next to me.'

'Let's assume you're right and the photo is doctored,' said Robbins. 'That still doesn't explain why a hitman would be looking for you, does it? And how can you be sure it's got nothing to do with what happened before?'

'I didn't say I was sure,' said Slater. 'You can never be sure, but why would they come back for me now? The case went stone cold almost straight away. Once we knew they'd all left the country, there was nothing we could do, so we went back to doing our normal jobs. We certainly haven't been looking for them. Anyway, you don't know it was going to be a hit. Like I said, maybe he was going to set me up for something.'

'I think the fact he had a car bomb suggests it was going to be a hit,' insisted Robbins. 'But whichever way you look at it, the question remains the same: who would have hired a Russian hit man to kill you or set you up?'

'I don't know.'

Robbins studied his face. 'Are you telling me you've never made any enemies? That's not what I understood.'

'Oh, I've made plenty of enemies,' said Slater.

'It's possible, then?'

'Well, yes, I suppose so. It's not something I've ever given a lot of thought to.'

'I think you need to start giving it some serious thought,' said Robbins. 'Because of who the dead man is, and because I know you have a habit of making enemies, I believe you were being hunted rather than set up in some way. But it would help if you could be a bit more forthcoming. You're not exactly making it easy for us.'

'I honestly don't know what to tell you,' said Slater. 'If you want me to write a list of enemies, it'll probably be a long one, but I'm not sure I could point the finger at anyone who would actually want to kill me.'

'I tell you what I'll do,' said Robbins. 'You make me a list of people who might want to get even with you, and we will speak to the airline about your girlfriend.'

Slater sighed. 'She's not my g—'

She smirked. 'Oh yes, sorry, I forgot, she's just a friend.'

'You need to speak to her,' said Slater. 'She's the one who might be able to tell you how my car came to be in

Winchester, and she might even remember if that guy, or anyone else, spoke to us in the airport lounge. And they must have CCTV at a secure police car park, mustn't they?'

'What about the list of enemies?'

'That's going to take a while. Can you give me an email address? I'll send it to you later today.'

She handed him a card. 'It's all on there,' she said. 'Email, phone and mobile. And if you think of anything else, I would like to know.'

'I'll give you a call if anything comes to mind,' he promised. 'And I'd appreciate it if you could keep me in the loop.'

She gave him a wry smile. 'You know there's not much I can tell you about an ongoing investigation.'

'Well, yeah, I know that, but even so,' said Slater.

'Right, we'll be off for now,' said Robbins, 'but don't think you've seen the last of us.'

CHAPTER TWELVE

After another frustrating night trying to contact Watson, Slater had struggled to get his mind back on the job, but Norman was aware of the situation and patiently reminded him what they were supposed to be doing, and why they were driving to a rendezvous with Peter Brooks, the ex-convict who claimed to have information about the Julie Harris murder.

'People like Brooks are a pet hate of mine,' Norman had warned Slater on the journey. 'Sneaking around conning old people out of their savings is about as low as it gets. Some of those people have had to sell their homes because of him.'

'If you're going to punch the guy, can you wait until after we've spoken to him, or am I going to have to restrain you?' asked Slater.

'I think I can probably wait,' said Norman, reluctantly.

'I understand you don't like the guy, but remember, he may have evidence to help our case. Assaulting him is unlikely to encourage him to share it with us.'

Norman mumbled something Slater didn't catch.

'At least he never physically hurt any of those old people.'

'He didn't need to,' said Norman. 'He ruined their lives and broke their hearts.'

'Are you sure it wouldn't be better if you waited in the car?'

'I promise I won't hit him, but don't expect me to act like I'm pleased to see him.'

'Okay, I can work with that,' said Slater. 'So how about I do the talking while you take notes? And try not to piss him off too much, at least not until we've got what we want.'

'He's a conman. The chances are this is a waste of time anyway,' said Norman, sulkily.

'Yeah, I'm aware of that, but don't forget, he didn't ask for money, did he?'

'He hasn't yet, but I wouldn't be at all surprised—'

'How about we stop trying to speak for him and wait and see what happens?' asked Slater. 'You never know, he might have become a reformed character.'

'How could we tell? The guy's a conman.'

Slater couldn't help but smile. He knew he wasn't going to win this one. 'Okay, I take your point, but we're here now, so we might as well find out what he has to say.'

Norman grunted a grudging acceptance of that fact.

* * *

Brooks had agreed to meet them in a quiet pub of his choice. After listening to Norman's rather graphic opinion of men like Peter Brooks throughout the entire thirty-minute journey, Slater had almost expected to find some creature that was perhaps half man and half snake. He hadn't anticipated the tall, smartly dressed, silver-haired sixty-something who rose elegantly from his chair and extended a hand in greeting.

Slater shook the hand as he made the introductions, but Norman kept his hands firmly in his pockets. If Brooks was offended by Norman's actions, he didn't show it except to incline his head slightly in acknowledgment. He indicated the chairs opposite his own, and they settled around the table.

'I understand you may find my presence offensive,' Brooks said, addressing Norman. 'What I did was very wrong, and I deeply regret doing it, but I have served my punishment, and I have recovered some of the money I stole and handed it back.'

Norman made to speak, but Brooks held up a hand. 'You don't have to tell me. I know it won't make up for the anguish I caused, but I'm doing all I can to make amends. That's why I'm here.'

'That's a great speech, but then what else would we expect a conman to say?' asked Norman.

Things weren't going quite as Slater had intended, and he cursed quietly under his breath as he kicked Norman under the table. 'We're not here to discuss what you did in the past, Mr Brooks,' he said. 'We're only interested in what you told Debbie Thomas you heard when you were in prison. Why don't you tell us about it?'

'As you probably know, I was supposed to serve four years in Lockstock Open Prison. In the event, I was released after two years, but while I was in there I spent some time in the company of a man who was completing a sentence. He spent the last year in Lockstock to prepare him for his return to the real world.'

'Does this man have a name?' asked Slater.

'His name was Scott Mulvaney.'

'Why was he inside?'

'I'm not sure exactly,' said Brooks, 'but it was something violent, which is why it seemed quite possible he was telling the truth about what he told me.'

'What exactly did he tell you?'

'I was reading a newspaper one day. There was a story about this man, Steve Harris, who was serving life for killing his wife in a caravan in Wales, and how his sister believed he was wrongly convicted and was still fighting to clear his name. Mulvaney came into the room and saw what I was reading.

'He said he thought Harris probably had been wrongly convicted because, around the time of her death, he had been offered fifty thousand pounds to kill a woman in a caravan in Wales. But it wasn't Harris who had offered him the money.'

'Did he do it?' asked Norman.

'He said he turned it down because he didn't agree with hurting women.'

'Did you believe him?'

'I could never quite decide, but he only ever said he was "offered" the money, and never that he had taken it.'

'When did he tell you this?' asked Slater.

'Three or four years ago.'

'And you've only just come forward now?'

'At the time, I thought he was probably trying to impress me and prove how hard he was, so I didn't think much of it. Then I saw the same story again a couple of months ago. At the end of the piece, it said they were appealing for anyone who had information that might help. That's when I remembered what Mulvaney had told me, so I contacted the newspaper.'

'Was that all he told you?' asked Slater. 'He didn't mention a name?'

'That's all I can recall. I'm sure I would have remembered if he had mentioned any names.'

Norman didn't look impressed. 'It's all a bit vague,' he said. 'How do we know this isn't more conman crap?'

'You don't,' admitted Brooks. 'But why would I lie? What could I possibly have to gain? It's not as if there's a reward or I'm asking for money.'

Much as Norman didn't like Brooks, he didn't argue the point any further.

'Do you have any idea where this Scott Mulvaney is?' asked Slater.

Brooks smiled indulgently. 'I may be a convicted criminal, Mr Slater, but Scott Mulvaney is a thug. I'm afraid he's not someone I would choose to include in my social circle. When I was released from prison, I had no desire to keep in touch with my fellow inmates, and I have no idea where any of them are.'

* * *

'That man is an arsehole of the finest order,' observed Norman as they headed for home.

'Really? You mean you don't like him? I would never have guessed,' said Slater.

'I don't shake hands with people like him.'

'Yes, I get it. I'm just pleased you didn't decide to shake him by the throat.'

'I was tempted.'

'But I'm pleased to say you didn't, so we live to fight another day,' said Slater. 'And he had a point, right? What has he got to gain by lying to us now?'

'He might think it's fun to waste our time.'

'But why would he? We've never met him before, and we didn't put him away. Besides, the newspaper must have thought he was okay.'

'I dunno,' said Norman. 'If they had thought there was a story in it, I'm sure they would have followed it up.'

'That's a good point,' admitted Slater, thoughtfully. 'But we can't be sure, can we?'

'I guess not.'

'So, what do you want to do, Norm, ignore it, or follow it up?'

'Much as I hate to admit it, we have no choice but to take it at face value for now,' conceded Norman. 'We'll have to try and find this Scott Mulvaney and see if he'll talk to us. I just hope it won't turn out to be a waste of time.'

CHAPTER THIRTEEN

It was just after seven p.m. Norman had insisted they sit down and compile a list of enemies as soon as they got back to the office, but it had taken much longer than they had expected. Making a list together had opened their eyes to the fact that although Slater had several possible suspects who would like to do him harm, Norman had even more.

They had just emailed it to Robbins and were now in Norman's car on their way home. 'I'm knackered,' said Slater.

'Yeah, me too,' agreed Norman. 'I didn't realise so many people might want to get their own back on me.'

'But most of those people would be happy just to punch us in the face,' said Slater. 'Planting a bomb is a bit extreme, don't you think?'

'And hiring an assassin to do the bomb-planting requires money,' added Norman. 'That sort of narrows the field down.'

'If we rule out the possibility this is linked to what happened before, I reckon there's only one real suspect, don't you?'

'Yeah, it has to be Bradshaw. But isn't he in prison on remand?'

'Yeah, but that doesn't make much difference, does it? A man with his contacts could still have ordered a hit. Maybe Robbins can find out who's been visiting him.'

They drove on in silence for a minute or two.

'Can I ask a question?' asked Norman.

'Sure.'

'I notice you've not exactly been honest with Robbins.'

'I haven't lied to her.'

'No, you haven't lied, but you haven't told her everything, have you? For instance, you didn't tell her you'd spoken to Watson.'

'She didn't ask me that. She asked if Watson had answered her phone, and she hasn't, so technically I didn't lie.'

Norman thought it was a moot point, but he wasn't going to argue about it. 'You didn't tell her Watson's address either. I thought you'd been there.'

'I've only been there once, and I was rather preoccupied. I didn't notice the address.'

'What exactly is this job of Watson's?'

'I'm beginning to wonder now,' said Slater. 'All she would tell me was that her base is in London, and my car was in a very secure police car park, guarded twenty-four seven.'

'Where is this car park?'

'She can't tell me.'

'What? Why not?'

'I have no idea,' said Slater.

'So, she's based in London, it's very secure, and she can't tell you any more than that,' mused Norman.

'That's what she said.'

'Sounds like she's some kind of spook.'

'You reckon? I hadn't even considered that, but then this whole situation is beginning to feel like some bizarre, surreal fantasy, so why not?'

'We used to come across those guys up in London sometimes,' said Norman. 'They never tell you anything, only that they're so special it's all way too secret to share with normal people like us. I didn't have much time for them myself.'

'Are you saying you think Watson works for MI5?'

Norman pursed his lips thoughtfully. 'Let's say I have my suspicions she's something more than just a run-of-the-mill cop. I've done nothing but think about this situation ever since our visitors left this morning. At first, I thought I was probably way off the mark, but now it's inside my head, I can't seem to shake it off, and the more I think about it, the more it seems possible.'

'But she was my DS. I would have known if she was a spy.'

'Why? I mean, no offence, but if she was working some undercover job and she was any good, what makes you think you would have known? Let's face it, you took her at face value, and why wouldn't you? I'm sure I would have too.'

'But we've just shared a hotel room for the best part of two weeks!'

'Yeah, but did she tell you anything about her new job? Did she even want to talk about work?'

'Well, no, now you come to mention it,' said Slater. 'We didn't talk about anything much, just vague stuff about nothing in particular.'

'And now she seems to want to put some distance between you, right?'

'But that's probably my fault for the way I reacted when she told me about her daughter.'

'Maybe, but not necessarily,' said Norman.

Slater sighed. He hadn't given it much thought before, but now Norm had mentioned it he couldn't seem to get past it. 'Come on then, Norm, let's hear this idea of yours.'

'Well, although you had no idea when you went to work for him, Bradshaw was a senior police officer who was pulling strings behind a couple of serious drug dealers, right?'

'Okay, but how does this make Watson a spy?'

'Hang on, I'm getting to that. When you took that job, it was a new department, right?'

'Yeah, it had just been set up.'

'And Watson was already there?'

'Yes. She was about to be invalided out, and Bradshaw rescued her career. When I joined, she had been working with him for a few months. She had helped him set up and get the thing off the ground.'

'Right. But thinking about it now, don't you think it was a bit odd Bradshaw had identified a relatively unknown DS with a busted knee as the person he needed to set up a new squad?'

'At the time I only had eyes for the chance of a new start,' said Slater. 'I saw no reason to question the set-up.'

'And there was no reason why you should,' said Norman. 'I mean, I didn't either. In fact, if you recall, I encouraged you to go for it.'

'What do you think now?'

'I have no proof, so this is just a theory, but what if Bradshaw was already under suspicion, and he was put in charge of this new squad so they could keep him out of the loop and keep an eye on him? Remember you told me once that you thought it was a sideways promotion for a guy with his ambitions.'

'And you think Watson was undercover, spying on him?'

'It's possible, don't you think? What if he didn't choose her, but someone recommended her to him and he couldn't say no?'

'But she was out working with me more than she was with him.'

'Yes, she was, but by then she had already been with him for a while and won his trust. Perhaps his reward for her efforts was to put her out with you. The thing is, she couldn't object because it would have looked suspicious if she had refused, wouldn't it? Anyway, I bet by the time you joined she had already gathered plenty of information about what he was up to, and he must have been under surveillance as well. Didn't she insist on being the one who went back to the office to do all the paperwork? That was probably just to keep an eye on him.'

Slater was beginning to feel pretty stupid. 'You're saying I worked with her for all that time and never suspected her once?'

'No, I'm saying she was brilliant at her job, and no one suspected her.'

Slater thought for a minute. 'Robbins and Wesley might have got this all wrong,' he said. 'If you're right about Watson being undercover and spying on Bradshaw, and he had found out, I might not be the target at all.'

'Yeah, you could well be right about that.'

'You saw that photo of Lenkov talking to Watson and me in the airport lounge in Thailand. What if he had gone to Thailand because he wanted me to lead him back to her? Maybe the photo was sent to someone to confirm it was her.'

'You think he was on your flight and followed Watson in your car, thinking it was her car?'

'I'm not exactly sure what I think, but it's possible, isn't it?'

CHAPTER FOURTEEN

On Saturday morning they made an extra early start. Slater was still brooding about the visit from DI Robbins, but the real reason for his dark mood was that Watson was continuing to ignore his calls. She hadn't spoken to him since she had hung up on him, but, as Norman had pointed out, there was nothing they could do about it right now, and anyway, they had a case of their own to investigate.

Their early start meant they made good time, and it was just after ten when they turned onto the shingle driveway that led up to 'Ivor Jones's' caravan site.

'Somehow, I was expecting something rather grander,' said Norman as he surveyed the slightly tatty-looking collection of caravans they could see.

'It's not exactly the Ritz, is it?' agreed Slater, his mood having mellowed during their four-hour journey. 'I'm having difficulty picturing someone like Harkness using a place like this. Maybe there are some bigger, better caravans somewhere else on the site.'

'Jeez, I hope so,' said Norman. 'But if there are, why put all this crap here where it's the first thing people see? It's put me off, and I wasn't even considering staying here.'

'And you can cancel my booking, that's for sure.'

They parked the car and made their way to what they assumed must be the site office. A smiley-faced girl of about eighteen jumped to her feet to greet them.

'You must be the detectives,' she said. 'If you'd like to follow me, Mr Jones is expecting you.'

She led them out of the office and along a narrow, hedge-lined path that seemed to go on forever. Eventually, they emerged onto a tarmac road lined at intervals with mobile homes. These were nothing like the shabby little caravans they had seen before.

'This is the executive area,' the girl explained. 'Mr Jones thought you would prefer to see him here where the murder happened.' She said the word 'murder' as if it might turn and bite her.

'He's in this first caravan, here,' she said, leading them up some steps onto an area of decking that surrounded the caravan. She knocked on the door and pushed it open.

'The detectives are here to see you, Ivor,' she called, indicating to Slater and Norman they should go in.

A small, grey-haired man welcomed them in. 'Do come in,' he said. 'You've had a long journey. I expect you could do with a cup of tea.'

'Now that sounds like a plan.' Norman looked curiously around the inside of the mobile home. It was definitely a lot smarter than the battered old caravans they'd seen on the way in.

'Is this the actual caravan where the murder took place?' asked Slater.

'This is the same pitch where the murder took place,' explained Jones. 'But it's not the same vehicle. We had always intended to improve this area, and it didn't seem right asking people to stay in a van where a murder had taken place, so we took the opportunity to remove all the old caravans from here and replace them with chalets. It made it a bit more upmarket.'

'That's a pity,' said Norman. 'It would have been good to get a feel for the area.'

'I'm sorry, but once the police said they'd finished with the scene, we couldn't wait to change it.'

'That's okay,' said Norman. 'I think we can understand that. We probably would have done the same.'

'It was a terrible thing.' Jones looked down at his hands. 'People stayed away. It took us three or four years to recover.'

Norman pulled a sheet of paper from the folder he had brought with him. 'According to the information we have here, there was maintenance scheduled for the caravan but it was never carried out. Is that right?'

There was a small briefcase on the floor by Jones's chair, and now he pulled a slim folder from it. 'You mentioned that when you called, so I went back through the records. I don't have the customer copy of the original order, but I do have our carbon copy, and I also have a copy of the telephone message that cancelled the order.'

He thumbed through the handful of sheets from the folder and handed two to Norman. 'These are copies I made. You can keep them if you like.'

Norman looked at the first carbon copy and handed it over to Slater. Then he took the second sheet and studied it.

It was a form headed *telephone message* and was obviously a standard form they had been using in the site office ten years ago. The message read, simply: *Please hold off on maintenance work until I notify you.* A name had been scrawled in the 'from' box. Norman studied the name, but the writing had been crammed in, and it was so faded, he couldn't decide what it said.

'I can't read that name,' he said, as he passed it over to Slater.

Slater studied the name, but he couldn't be sure either.

'It was ten years ago now, and I can't be sure,' Jones said, 'but Julie used to be the one who dealt with us all the time, so we took it to be J Harris.'

'Did you take the message?' asked Slater.

'No, it would have been my wife. She was running the office back then.'

'Maybe we could ask her?'

'I'm afraid you'd need a seance to do that, Mr Slater,' said Jones, ruefully. 'My wife died four years ago.'

'Oh, I'm sorry,' said Slater, awkwardly.

'That's okay, you weren't to know. But I'm afraid she can't help you now.'

'Was the site closed at the time of the murder?' asked Norman.

'Well, officially, yes.' Jones looked down at his hands again. 'The local council insists we have to close to qualify as a holiday site. If we allow access to the caravans for more than nine months of the year, we become classed as a residential site, and then we'd have to abide by a whole new set of rules.'

'What do you mean by "officially" closed?' asked Slater.

'Back then we used to turn a blind eye to anyone who wanted to come for a weekend as long as they were discreet.'

'So, if someone wanted to come for a dirty weekend?' asked Norman.

'We weren't always here, and we never used to ask why they were here.'

'So, they could have been?'

'If we were here and we saw them, we didn't ask. As long as people were discreet, we turned a blind eye. We certainly didn't go spying on people to see what they were up to.'

'Did you keep records of who was here unofficially?' asked Slater.

'No, we didn't. Anyway, we stopped all that after the murder.'

'Did people pay for these unofficial visits?'

'No.' Jones shook his head firmly. 'I kept no records, and I took no money. It was like a perk for those who owned their caravans and kept them on this site.'

'And you were never notified to carry out the maintenance work?' asked Norman.

'No.'

'Didn't you chase them up about it?' asked Slater. 'I thought that was when all that sort of work was supposed to be carried out.'

'We have a hundred caravans of our own to service and thirty-eight belonging to owners. I used to do all the maintenance myself. If someone told me to hold off, I was only too happy to have one less to look after. Besides, if they ask for maintenance outside those three months, I can charge them extra.'

'You prefer not to chase them,' said Slater.

'Wouldn't you?' asked Jones. 'To be honest, I wish I had chased them. Have you ever been near a body that's been dead for a few weeks? Jesus, the stink . . .'

CHAPTER FIFTEEN

'This is getting to be a habit,' said Slater, as Robbins and Wesley came through the door late on Saturday afternoon.

'One that I could do without, quite frankly,' said Robbins. 'I'd much rather be working in Winchester where I know my way around.' She looked around. 'I know it's a bit cheeky, but d'you mind if I use your loo?'

'It's through there.' Slater pointed to a door across the office. 'It's a bit basic. We haven't got around to finishing the decorating yet.'

Robbins pulled a face. 'Is it clean?'

'Yes.'

She headed for the door. 'Good,' she said over her shoulder. 'I don't mind basic, as long as it's clean.'

As the door closed behind her, Slater and Wesley stared at each other. 'So, what brings you here today?' asked Slater.

'I take it you still haven't managed to get in touch with the elusive DS Brearley?'

'I'm afraid not. I have no idea where she is.'

'Really?' The suspicion was clear in Wesley's voice.

'I'm beginning to think the last few months of my life must have been a dream.'

'A good one?'

'I thought so at the time, but now I think it was a nightmare in disguise.'

'Well, it's about to get worse.'

Slater sighed. 'How does that work?'

'Can you tell me where you were on Tuesday night, say between ten and one?'

'Asleep, in my bed,' said Slater.

'Can anyone verify that?'

'I'm afraid not.'

Wesley sniffed disapprovingly. 'Have you thought about why Lenkov might have wanted to kill you?'

'I told you, I have no idea.'

'Or perhaps you know exactly why,' said Wesley, with a smug grin, 'and you killed him before he could kill you.'

Slater studied the young DS. 'Is this why I need an alibi? Are you suggesting I was there and somehow detonated the bomb as he got out from under the car?'

Wesley said nothing but looked immensely pleased with himself.

'Sorry,' said Slater, 'but you've lost me. I thought your theory was that Lenkov detonated the bomb himself, accidentally, while he was planting it.'

'It was, but now we've changed our minds. It makes sense when you think about it. The guy was supposed to be something of an expert with car bombs, so he would be the last person to make a stupid mistake and blow himself up.'

'So, you think someone waited for him to plant his bomb, and then blew him up? How could they do that?'

'Remote control.'

Slater thought for a second. 'But that means—'

'Someone watched Lenkov plant his bomb and then pressed a button?' Wesley smiled coldly. 'That's the most likely way. It's not looking too good for you, is it?'

Slater looked at Wesley as though he were deranged. 'You seriously think I killed him?' he asked, incredulously. 'That would require some serious technical know-how, and anyone will tell you that's not in my remit.'

'I think someone killed him that night, and you don't have an alibi.'

'Most of the people who live alone in this town won't have an alibi,' said Slater. 'And why would I kill him? I didn't even know he existed until you showed me his photograph.'

'Well, that's what you've told us,' said Wesley.

The door opened across the room and Robbins appeared. She stared at the two men, immediately reading their body language. Suddenly, Wesley didn't look quite so sure of himself.

'What's going on?' she asked.

'You'd better ask young Sherlock here.' Slater jerked his thumb at Wesley. 'He seems to think he's going to put me away for murder.'

Robbins looked hard at Wesley. 'I told you to wait for me, didn't I?'

'Yes, but—'

'You know, Wesley,' said Slater, 'you really should listen to your boss when she tells you to put that spade down and keep quiet.'

Wesley looked puzzled. 'Spade? What spade?'

'The one you're using to dig yourself a bloody great hole. I don't give a damn that you don't like me, but I can tell you now, you're going to be wasting a lot of your time, and hers, if you continue trying to make your evidence fit me.'

'Is that right?' said Wesley, the smug grin back on his face. 'So how do you explain being photographed driving your car into Winchester on Tuesday night from the Tinton direction?'

Across the room, Norman was pottering about making tea, but he froze as Wesley spoke. As for Slater, he had been caught completely off guard. How the hell could he have been photographed driving his car anywhere that night? Would Watson have driven down to Winchester? She had assured him she hadn't moved the car. Surely, she would have told him first.

Norman spun around to see Slater's mouth flapping wordlessly. He obviously didn't know what to say, but

Wesley was so pleased with himself he completely missed the chance to catch Slater out and instead began speaking again.

'We checked on ANPR, and sure enough, it comes into the city at 23.05.'

'And you're quite sure it was Dave's car, and he was driving it?' asked Norman.

'Who else would it have been?'

'Ah! You're not sure, are you? Can you show us the photos?' Norman moved across to stand next to Slater. 'That would show the number plate, right? And with any luck, we can see the driver, too. Trust me — if it shows Dave in the driver's seat, I'll hand him over to you myself.'

The smile disappeared from Wesley's face and his confidence visibly evaporated. 'Er, well, I don't think we can do that,' he began.

Robbins stepped forward, placing a hand on his arm to warn him into silence. 'It's alright, Wesley. I think you can leave this to me.' She turned to Norman. 'For some reason, the number plate isn't clear. And we haven't got a shot that identifies the driver.'

Norman was on a roll now and he wasn't going to stop. 'So, all you have is a blurred photograph of a car, that's a similar model and colour to Dave's, that could be his but could as easily belong to someone else. You also have no idea who's driving, or even if it's a man or a woman. Am I right?'

Robbins nodded.

'Now, I don't want to tell you guys how to do your jobs,' continued Norman, 'but I think we've all been detectives long enough to agree this might be enough to give you grounds for suspicion, but it proves nothing.'

'Yes, of course.' Robbins held her hands up. 'I think I've allowed my colleague to get a bit carried away, and I apologise for that, but we were all young and keen once, weren't we?'

'So, am I accused of murder, or what?' asked Slater.

'I understand how you must feel, Mr Slater,' said Robbins, looking him right in the eye. 'But you know how it is. I have to dot the "i"s, and cross the "t"s, and at the moment you can't explain why this man had your details and photos, and you have no alibi.'

Slater studied her face for a few seconds. 'But you don't really believe I murdered him, do you?'

She made a face that suggested it was in the balance but then gave a half smile. 'You know I can't just dismiss you as a suspect with all these loose ends, don't you?'

Slater nodded. 'Yeah, I understand. You need to make sure.'

'As I said before, you're not exactly making it easy for us, are you?'

'And as I said before, I honestly don't know what to tell you,' said Slater.

'Well, what about your car? If you didn't drive it to Winchester, how did it come to be parked in that car park?'

'I told you, I loaned it to DS Brearley when we got back from Thailand.'

'Oh, yes, you trusted your girlfriend with your almost new Range Rover.'

'She's not my girlfriend,' said Slater, patiently, 'and why does everyone find it so surprising? It's just a car.'

Robbins smiled. 'Spoken like a true millionaire. But you're wrong. It's not "just a car" — it's fifty grand's worth of car!'

'Yes, alright, if you want to put it like that.' Slater shrugged. 'But it's in the hands of a police officer who has all the advanced driver training you can think of.'

'Is that what she told you?'

'Look, she used to drive the car when we worked together. I'd trust her with my gold-plated Rolls Royce if I had one.'

'The thing is, we still haven't been able to find her.'

'What about the airline?'

'Oh, they confirm someone using that name was on the plane, and they confirm she was sitting next to you, but after that, she vanishes into thin air. There's no trace of her anywhere.'

'She can't be here one minute and then completely disappear,' said Slater.

Robbins' mobile phone was ringing. She pulled it from her pocket and looked at the screen. 'Excuse me,' she said. 'I need to take this.'

She retreated to the other side of the office and spoke into the phone for about thirty seconds then came back to join them. She looked distinctly uncomfortable but was trying not to show it.

'That was my boss,' she said. 'Something's come up. We have to go.'

'That's a bit sudden,' said Slater.

'Yes, well, you know how it is. Orders are orders. Come on, Wesley.'

CHAPTER SIXTEEN

Slater and Norman watched as Robbins and Wesley climbed into their car and drove off. 'That was a weird way to end an interview,' said Slater. 'D'you think they got called to something more important, or they just got called off?'

'Robbins looked pretty miffed,' said Norman. 'And wouldn't the control room be the ones calling for them to go to another job?'

'You think they were called off?'

'Can't say for sure, but that's how it looked to me.'

'Yeah, but why?'

Norman shook his head. 'I have no idea, but I'm beginning to think your friend Watson must have something to do with this.'

'Watson? You think so?'

'If she is some kind of spook and Robbins is getting too close to what actually happened, maybe someone up high has decided it's time to call a halt before it gets embarrassing for them.'

Slater stared at Norman. 'Do you think she really is?'

'Look, if what Robbins says is true and she was on that flight as Samantha Brearley and then suddenly doesn't exist, it's the only explanation.' Norman took in the look on

Slater's face. 'Look, I know you don't want to admit it, but it's the only thing that makes sense. I know you were worried she might have been a victim herself, and that would explain why no one could find her, but it wouldn't explain how her identity has been wiped away, would it?'

Slater sunk his head into his hands. 'I feel such a bloody fool.'

'If it's any consolation, I don't think she set out to mislead you, but what choice did she have? If Bradshaw appointed you, she would have had no way of knowing if she could trust you. Maybe whoever she works for told her to keep her distance.'

'But she didn't, though, did she? We shared a bed in Thailand!'

'Didn't you enjoy those ten nights?'

'Well, yeah, I did as it happens.'

'Instead of feeling used, why don't you accept it for what it was? If I'd spent the best part of two weeks in the sun with a woman like that, I think I'd be feeling pretty grateful!'

Slater let out a strangled cough.

'Okay, look, that's not exactly what I meant,' said Norman. 'Obviously she wouldn't want to spend ten nights with an old fart like me. Jeez, I'd probably have another heart attack! I just think you shouldn't make it into something it isn't. I don't know her well, but even so, I'm pretty sure she likes you and has a lot of time for you. What you have to think about is: how could she have told you she wasn't who you thought she was after all this time?'

Slater thought about this. It was something he hadn't considered. 'I suppose it would be difficult.'

'Difficult? If I'm right about her, it's her job to be someone she isn't. Can you imagine yourself in that position? It must be impossible to play two people at once, so maybe she stays in character all the time, as some actors do.'

'I suppose you've got a point.'

'I should think it makes it almost impossible to have a proper relationship with anyone.'

'Yeah, but she didn't have to lead me on,' Slater said miserably.

'I don't think she meant to. If it was the other way around, wouldn't you have still found her attractive?'

'Well, yeah.'

'And that's what I think happened. Didn't you tell me it was a case of two consenting adults who fancied spending some time together in the sun? No strings attached.'

'I suppose when you put it like that, I can't really complain, but I still feel like an idiot.'

Norman shrugged. 'Okay, so, feel like a lucky idiot.'

Slater couldn't think of an answer to that, so he changed the subject. 'What do you think about my car getting caught on ANPR driving into Winchester?'

'We don't know it was your car. Maybe it's a car that looks like yours. Anyway, if it's the one that blew up, it had to get into that car park somehow.'

'It's unusual for the number plates not to show up, though. That's the whole point of these cameras, isn't it?'

'Maybe someone put some sort of reflective tape over them to disguise them.'

Slater considered this. 'Yeah, but why drive it there in the first place? If Lenkov was after me, he had my address, so why plant a bomb under the car and then take it to Winchester? It makes no sense.'

'I think you got it right last night and they've got this whole thing wrong,' said Norman. 'I mean, if you were going to plant a car bomb, you'd make sure the person you were trying to kill was going to be the one to detonate it, right?'

'Exactly. That theory only works if I drive into Winchester and Lenkov follows me, watches me park and walk off, and then plants the bomb before I get back. Then, when I switch the ignition on, boom!'

'Or he detonates it remotely,' said Norman. 'Either way, you have to be there.' A frown slowly creased his face. 'But then it would be the same if Watson was the target, wouldn't it?'

'Perhaps he stole the car and was planning to tip me off with an anonymous phone call.'

'But if that's the case, why not leave the car in Tinton? Why Winchester?' asked Norman. 'And if he's after Watson and he stole it in London, why drive all the way down here? Now I'm not sure it makes sense either way.'

'And another thing. If he stole it, why did she insist it was still where she left it?' asked Slater. 'Why not tell me? She knows I'm not going to make a big deal out of it. Cars get stolen, that's why we have insurance.'

They were silent for a couple of minutes while they thought things over. It was Slater who broke the silence. 'So, we're agreed the police have got it wrong.'

'We are.'

'Are we also agreed that we haven't got a better idea?'

'We are.'

'Are you getting a headache thinking about this?'

'I am. I suggest we knock off, go home, and think about something else.'

'That sounds like a plan,' said Slater. 'Tomorrow is another day, right?'

'Ah, yeah, about that.' Norman turned faintly pink. 'I'm not going to be around much for the rest of this weekend. I promised Jane I'd take her and the kids out somewhere.'

Slater smiled. 'That's okay. What time are you heading off?'

'Well, actually, I was thinking of heading off about now. If I'm quick, I can get there in time to see the kids before they go to bed.'

CHAPTER SEVENTEEN

Left to his own devices, Slater had worried about Watson all night. Suppose she was the target; did that mean she was safe now Lenkov was dead, or would someone else come after her? Either way, he had come to the conclusion he had to speak to her, and if she wouldn't answer his phone calls, he figured maybe there was another way.

It was just before ten a.m. when he finally reached his destination. He asked the taxi driver to wait and agreed to meet him at a nearby cafe, then he walked up to the front door to her flat. He rang the bell, readying his best smile, but when the door opened, his smile disappeared. The woman standing before him looked a bit like Watson, but her hair was darker, and she wasn't quite as tall.

'Yes? Can I help you?' she asked.

His mouth flapped wordlessly once or twice. He had been sure this was the right flat. 'I'm sorry, I think I must have the wrong address. I was looking for Sam Brearley.'

The woman frowned and studied him suspiciously for a few seconds as if she hadn't heard him correctly. 'Who?'

'Samantha Brearley.'

She still looked puzzled, but then she suddenly seemed to understand what he had said. 'Oh, yes, of course, Sam. Was she expecting you?'

'Er, no. I've been trying to reach her all week, but all I get is her voicemail. I was starting to get a bit worried about her, so I thought I'd better come and see if she was okay.'

She continued to study him as if she was making her mind up about something. 'She won't be happy about this, you know. She doesn't like people checking up on her.'

Slater felt his cheeks begin to redden. 'I'm not checking up on her. I'm a friend, and I was worried about her.'

'She won't like that either. She's quite capable of looking after herself.'

'I used to work with her, so I know how capable she is. I was concerned, that's all.'

'Hang on a minute. Was she in Thailand with you?'

'That's right, yes.'

'And you let her take your car?'

'Yes.'

At last, her face broke into a familiar smile. 'You must be Dave,' she said. 'I'm Sam's sister, Mel.'

'So, does that mean I have got the right address?'

'In a manner of speaking.'

Slater frowned. He wasn't quite sure what she meant by that, but before he could ask, she spoke again. 'She didn't tell you, then?'

'Tell me what?'

'You'd better come in. I think I probably need to explain.'

She stepped back to let him in.

'Need to explain what?' he asked as he made his way past her into the flat.

'I'm afraid my sister's a lovely girl, but she's not very good at relationships,' she said as she led him through to the living room.

'Yes, well, it's not exactly my superpower,' confessed Slater.

A small blonde girl Slater guessed must be about seven years old was watching a cartoon on the TV. She turned her head as he came into the room. 'Who's he?'

'This is Dave.'

'Hello, Dave, how are you?' asked the girl.

'Hi. I'm very well, thank you. What's your name?'

'I'm Trudy.'

'That's a nice name.'

'Why, thank you,' said the girl, and beamed a big gap-toothed smile at him.

'Right, young lady,' Mel said to the girl. 'I'm going to make Dave a cup of tea, but in fifteen minutes I want to see you out of those pyjamas, teeth cleaned, ready to go to karate class. Okay?'

'Okay.' Trudy turned off the TV and set off upstairs to get ready.

'She's cute,' said Slater as he followed Mel into the kitchen.

'Yeah, she's a little angel really,' said Mel.

'Is she yours?'

'Sam and I sort of share her.'

Slater looked confused.

'We had another sister, Suzie, but we lost her three years ago. Trudy was her daughter. Sam and I vowed we'd look after her when her mum died. It was difficult at first, but we've got it figured out now.'

'What happened to Suzie?'

'She was a detective sergeant in the police. She was killed by a car bomb.'

'Bloody hell,' whispered Slater. 'We all know it could happen, but when it does . . . Jesus. I had no idea. Sam never mentioned it.'

'No, she wouldn't.'

'When she told me she had a daughter, I assumed—'

'Oh no, she's never had any kids of her own. Trudy's adopted.'

'I got that completely wrong then,' said Slater. 'I had no idea.'

She gave him a wistful smile. 'Don't worry. You thought what she wanted you to think.'

'I'm sorry?'

'She told it the way she did to put you off. She likes you, but the last thing she wants is a serious relationship. She knows from experience that you tell most blokes you've got a daughter and they're off like a shot.'

Slater would have been quite happy if the ground had opened up and swallowed him right there and then. 'Well, I can't deny I was a bit surprised,' he conceded.

'Shock, horror,' said Mel. 'That's what you're supposed to feel.'

'But I worked with her for months. Why didn't she tell me before?'

'Like I said, she doesn't want to get involved with anyone right now. All she wants to do is find out who killed her sister.'

'You mean no one was convicted?'

'No one was even questioned. It seemed to be completely random, as if Suzie was some guinea pig and someone did it just to see if they could.'

All the time Mel had been speaking, she had kept an eye on the door, and now she made a face at Slater as Trudy came bouncing back down the stairs and ran across to the kitchen.

'Let me see those pearly whites,' said Mel

Trudy obediently opened wide, and Mel carried out a thorough inspection. 'Oh, my, they're so bright I'm almost blinded,' she announced. 'Have you got your kit ready?'

'It's all in the bag ready to go.'

'Good girl. Now, do I get a hug and a kiss?'

She got down on her knees, so Trudy could place her arms around her neck. They exchanged a big hug and a kiss. 'Can you watch a bit more TV while I finish talking to Dave?'

'Okay.'

As the small girl made her way back to her TV cartoon, Slater fought to control the lump that seemed to be trying to fill his throat. 'I came here once before,' he said, 'but you and Trudy weren't here.'

'We have a chalet down on the coast. We spend a lot of time there.'

'It must be difficult with Sam being away so much.'

'I'm always here. We decided I would work part-time so Sam could work at finding who killed our sister. It's our way of sharing the load. When she's home for a couple of weeks, I get my "me" time.'

She made a point of looking at her watch. 'We have to go. I've got to get Trudy to her karate class.' She started tidying things away.

'Right. Of course,' said Slater. 'D'you know where Sam is right now or what she's doing? As I said, I've been trying to reach her.'

'I don't ask,' said Mel. 'What I don't know about, I don't worry about.'

'Does she keep in touch?'

'As often as she can.'

'Can you pass on a message? Can you tell her I called and ask her to call me? I wouldn't ask, but it's essential.'

'If she calls, I'll tell her, but I warn you — she won't be happy you've been here.'

'Tell her if she answered her phone I wouldn't have had to come here.'

Mel had slipped a jacket on now, and she jingled her car keys. Slater knew a hint when he saw one.

'I'll get out of your way,' he said, as he made his way towards the front door. 'Thanks for the tea.'

'Trudy, say goodbye to Dave.'

Trudy turned to Slater. 'Goodbye, Dave. It was nice meeting you.'

'Goodbye, Trudy.'

CHAPTER EIGHTEEN

It was one thirty on Sunday afternoon and Slater's mobile phone was ringing. Bleary-eyed, he dragged himself from a deep sleep into which he'd plunged on coming back from meeting Trudy and Mel.

'Is that Mr Slater?'

'It is.'

'This is PC Weston from Tinton Police Station.'

'What can I do for you, Weston? You know I don't work for the police any more, don't you?'

'Yes, sir. I do know. I just thought you'd like to know we've found your car.'

Slater thought he must have got that wrong. 'You've what?'

'Found your car, sir. I understood it was reported missing.'

Slater was struggling to get his brain engaged after his nap, coupled with a late case of jet lag. 'It was? I mean, yes, it was. Where is it?'

'It's down at Tinton Railway Station, in the car park.'

'Is it still in one piece?'

'If you mean has it been jacked up and the wheels removed, I'm happy to report no, it hasn't. It looks to be in perfectly good condition, but I think it may have been here for some days — there are several parking tickets plastered to the windscreen.'

'Are you going to tow it away? Where will it be? When can I collect it?'

'Between you and me, sir, it would make life much easier for us if you just come and collect it from here. You have a spare key, I assume?'

'Yes, I've got a spare. And you're sure the car's okay?'

'It looks fine to me, but if anything is missing or damaged you can, of course, report it, and we'll look into it.'

Slater knew very well that car crime was way down the list of priorities for a hard-pressed officer, so he wasn't surprised by the offer. 'I'm going to have to walk down there to get it, and I'm a bit . . . um . . . busy, so I'll be about an hour.'

'That's okay, sir, I wasn't planning on waiting.'

'No, don't,' said Slater. 'I'm sure you've got plenty to do without playing nursemaid to my car. Thanks for letting me know.'

Slater ended the call, climbed from bed, and made his way to the bathroom. What the hell was his car doing in Tinton? And could it really be in perfect condition? This situation was getting weirder by the day.

* * *

Twenty minutes later and he had showered, dressed and was ready to go. Then his doorbell rang. Muttering under his breath about people ringing his bell on a Sunday afternoon, he opened the door.

'Bloody hell,' he said. 'Just when I thought my day couldn't get any more weird.'

'And good afternoon to you,' said DI Stella Robbins.

Slater looked over her shoulder, but there was no Wesley. 'Are you on your own?'

'On my own,' she said.

'Then I suppose you'd better come in.' He stepped back to allow her through the door. 'I take it this is about the case?' he said, following her inside.

'Well, it's funny you should say that,' said Robbins. 'Only there is no case.'

'What?'

'Remember I took a call when I was with you yesterday? I've been ordered to close my investigation and hand over all my evidence. Even the wrecked car has gone.'

'Taken away by whom?'

'Officially I don't know, but I can make a pretty good guess.'

'So that's what that phone call was. We thought you left rather abruptly.'

'I was wondering if perhaps you have friends in high places.'

Slater couldn't stop himself chuckling. 'Who, me? I've probably got one or two enemies up there, but I'm not the "friends in high places" type.'

'Well, someone pulled the plug on my case, and you were the only person we had spoken to.'

'Is this an official visit?' asked Slater.

'Good God, no. As I said, I no longer have a case to investigate. Officially, I have no reason to speak to you.'

'You're taking a bit of a risk, then, aren't you? I mean, if it was me who stopped the case, I could easily drop you right in the crap now, couldn't I?'

'You could if it was you,' said Robbins. 'But if I thought you were the sort who would do that I wouldn't be here.'

'So, let me get this right,' said Slater. 'You're here, in your own time, because you want to know why your case has been closed down, is that it?'

'That's about the size of it.'

'Why me?'

'Who else am I going to turn to?'

'But what makes you think I can help?'

'Because you're involved in all this somehow. I just haven't figured out how.'

'I told you I have no idea who Lenkov was, and I don't know why someone used a car just like mine to kill him.'

Robbins studied Slater's face and then smiled. 'My DS might be a bit green, Mr Slater, but I'm not a fool. You know a lot more than you've been letting on, and while I don't believe you've tried to kill anyone, I'm pretty sure you're as keen as I am to know why someone has used a car with cloned number plates to blow up Yuri Lenkov.'

'Cloned number plates? You didn't tell me that before.'

'I didn't know until yesterday. I made a point of catching up with Forensics before I handed everything over. I learned some fascinating stuff.'

'I take it your car's outside?'

'I did think about using my broomstick, but it's warmer in the car.'

'Then would you give me lift? I've got to pick something up from the railway station.'

'Yes, but—'

'Trust me — you're going to want to see it. We can talk on the way.'

* * *

'So, what did you learn?' asked Slater, as Robbins drove him away from his house.

'The forensics team think there was already a bomb under the car when Lenkov planted his bomb. Someone detonated it while he was next to the car.'

'Ah, so that explains it.'

'Explains what?'

'We were talking about this after you left yesterday. We thought someone must have been watching Lenkov plant his bomb and then, somehow, they had detonated it remotely, but we couldn't see how you would do that. But, of course, if there were another bomb hidden away, it would have detonated his at the same time.'

'I can tell you something else, too,' said Robbins. 'We confirmed it wasn't your car. When they eventually checked the VIN against the DMV database, they could see it was a car exactly like yours, but not yours. The number plates were cloned.'

Slater was tempted to tell her he already knew it wasn't his car, but he didn't want to spoil the surprise. 'Where did the car come from?'

'We didn't get that far, but my guess is it was stolen. I can check that out, but I wanted to keep my head down for a day or two. I intend to check all the CCTV footage I can find as well. Someone drove that car into Winchester, and if one ANPR camera caught it, there must be others, too.'

Slater thought it was only fair that if Robbins was prepared to share information, he should too. 'If we're sharing information, you should know we think Samantha Brearley could be working for MI5.'

Robbins stared straight ahead. 'That would explain a lot. She'll be the one with friends in high places then. How long have you known?'

'I know it sounds unlikely, but I worked with her for months and never suspected a thing. It was Norman who suggested the possibility. He thinks she was working undercover when we met, and she couldn't tell me because she didn't know if she could trust me.'

Robbins was smiling now. 'You mean you went to Thailand with someone who wasn't who she said she was?'

Slater felt his cheeks glowing. 'I admit it's embarrassing, but I had no reason to question who she was.'

'But was it worth it?'

'I don't think that's relevant, do you?' he said.

Robbins pursed her lips thoughtfully. 'Can I hear the sound of a gentleman being discreet?'

'I couldn't possibly say.'

'Good grief, it is, isn't it? What a refreshing change!' Robbins turned her car into Station Road. 'Right, we're here. Where do you want me to go?'

'The car park,' said Slater, pointing to their left. 'Over there.'

Robbins followed his directions. 'We're not stopping, are we?'

'Not for long,' he said, pointing to a Range Rover ahead of them. 'Right there will do.'

'Wait a minute. Is that . . . ?'

'My car? Yes, apparently it's been here for days.'

'But it can't have been. I put out a priority search for it on Wednesday afternoon.'

'Yeah, maybe,' said Slater, easing his door open, 'but the station car park wouldn't be where you'd expect to find it, would it? They only spotted it this morning because they always do a tour of the station on Sunday mornings.'

Robbins stopped the car and jumped out with him. 'Careful, it could be booby-trapped.'

'I don't think so, do you?' he said, pointing at the windscreen, which had several parking tickets attached. 'It's been here for days looking at that lot.'

Slater was quite confident the car would be safe, but even so, he got down on his knees and made a cursory inspection underneath before he unlocked the car.

'Before you press the button on that key fob, can we stand back a bit?' Robbins asked nervously.

'Now you've brought this subject up, there's something I wanted to ask. Why didn't you call the bomb squad the other night?'

'Two reasons: first, I figured if there had been a booby trap it would have detonated with the bomb. Second, If I had called them, they would have called MI5, and I wouldn't have got a look in. It was my case. Why should I let them take over?'

'You're right. I would have done the same,' agreed Slater.

'I still think we need to be careful here, though.'

Slater scoffed. 'Do you honestly think that's necessary?'

'At least let's use my car as a shield.' Robbins moved across to her car, but Slater was still unconvinced.

'I know you think I'm overdramatic,' she said, 'but humour me, will you?'

He gave her a wry smile and joined her behind her car. 'You might want to get your head down,' he said. 'I tell you what, why don't I do a countdown?'

'This isn't funny,' she said. 'It's less than a week since I last had to deal with scattered body parts.'

Slater conceded the point. 'Okay, fair enough, but I'm sure you're wrong.' He raised the key fob so she could see it. 'Right here goes then: five, four, three, two, one . . . Boom!'

There was a soft popping noise as the doors unlocked. Robbins looked up at Slater's grinning face from her position crouching down behind her car.

'Oh, ha, ha, very funny,' she said. 'You could have got your head blown off.'

'Maybe it's wired to the ignition. Stay there a minute while I check.'

'No, wait,' she began, but it was too late, he was already swinging the door open and climbing into the driver's seat, easing it back to its full extent.

He grinned at her and pushed the start button. Sure enough, the engine roared to life.

'There you go,' he called. 'Good as gold.'

'That was bloody stupid, and reckless,' she said, walking across to the car. 'You had no idea if it was safe. You could have been—'

'You're just annoyed because I was right,' said Slater. 'Now jump in and see if you can find any evidence.'

'Evidence of what?'

'Who drove it here for a start.'

'It was a woman,' she said with certainty.

He looked at her enquiringly, and she returned his look with a satisfied smile.

'You just pushed the seat way back,' she said.

'Ha!' he said. 'You've done this sort of thing before, haven't you?'

'Do you always joke about everything?'

'Hey, look, there was a time when I thought I was the most hard-done-by bloke in the world and I used to take everything seriously. Then I met a guy called Norman. Now there's a guy who's had some serious crap to deal with, and yet he can still see the funny side of most things. I thought, if he can find a way to deal with all his shit and still smile, then so can I.'

'So now everything's a joke, is it?'

'Of course not, but you've got to keep it all in perspective. I mean, there's always someone in a worse situation, isn't there?'

'There is?'

'Take the other night,' Slater continued. 'You probably thought it couldn't get much worse when you found that Russian guy with his legs blown off, but it could have been much worse. You could have been him, couldn't you?'

'I suppose when you put it like that.'

'Every cloud has a silver lining.'

'And that works for you, does it?'

'You didn't go home and cry your eyes out after you found Lenkov, did you?'

'I took my mum's dog for a long walk.'

'And I bet you do that every time you get a shit situation,' said Slater. 'It's how you cope, right? We all have to find a way to deal with it or we'd never survive. You walk your mum's dog; I try not to take it too seriously.'

'And does it work?'

'Most of the time, but not always,' he admitted. They carried on searching in silence until Slater spoke again. 'There's sod all of any use here, is there?'

'Nada,' she agreed.

'What do we do now?'

'What do you want to do?'

'I'd like to find out why someone needed to use a copy of my car to kill a man called Lenkov.'

'But all my evidence has been taken away, and we've been warned off.'

'You're the one who's been warned off,' said Slater, 'not me.'

'You could get your girlfriend into trouble.'

'How many more times do I have to tell you — she's not my girlfriend.'

'Alright, but you could get yourself into trouble.'

'Me and trouble are old friends, and anyway, with the resources at my disposal these days there's no guarantee I can get anywhere near the truth.'

'I've got resources,' Robbins said.

Slater turned to look at her. She met his gaze and held it. 'I don't think you should get involved.'

'What, are you my dad now? I'm a big girl. I've been making my own decisions for a long time.'

'You'd be taking a big risk.'

She nodded to acknowledge the truth in his statement. 'I don't like the idea of someone being able to walk into my town, blow someone's legs off, and then sweep it all under the carpet as if it never happened.'

'They would tell you a man like Lenkov got what he deserved.'

'And they might even be right,' she said, 'but I still want to know who did it, and why they needed to come to Winchester to do it.'

'I'll bet it was a random choice. Stick a pin in a map, anywhere outside London.'

She pulled a face. 'I'd like to think it was something better than that.'

'A tenner says I'm right.'

'God, I hope you're not.'

'Does this mean we're a team?' he asked.

'I think that might be taking it a bit too far. Anyway, I thought you were already in a team. What's Norman going to think about this? Aren't you supposed to be working with him?'

'If I know Norm, he'll be happy to get involved as well.'

'Don't you have a case already?'

'Yeah, but we should be able to work both. It's not as if we're going to be able to work very fast on this, is it? If we raise our heads too high above the parapet, they'll be onto us straight away.'

Slater looked at his watch, jumped out of the car, picked all the parking tickets off his windscreen, and climbed back in. She reached out a hand, and he gave her the tickets. She quickly looked through them.

'How about a strategy meeting?' he asked.

'What?'

'Strategy, you know, how we're going to do this.'

'Yes, I know what strategy is, thank you. I was looking at these parking tickets. They don't look right to me. What do you think?'

She passed one of the tickets back to him, and he stared at it. 'Sorry. Traffic management was never my field.'

'Can I take them with me?'

'Be my guest. You can pay the fines for me if you like. Anyway, strategy meeting.'

'What have you got in mind?' she asked, suspiciously.

'Have you had any lunch? Only I haven't, and I'm starving. I know a place that does a fantastic all-day roast.'

She studied his face. At least he hadn't suggested they went back to his place. 'I am hungry.'

'Come on then, park your car and jump in. I'm paying.'

She parked her car, climbed into the passenger seat, and settled back into the comfortable leather seat.

'So, this is how rich people live,' she said, admiring the interior of the car, as Slater pulled away.

He shrugged. 'It gets me from A to B.'

'Oh, come on,' she said, 'this is one tasty motor. Don't tell me you don't enjoy driving it!'

He smiled at her. 'I'd be a liar if I said it was run of the mill, but at the end of the day, it is just a car.'

She laughed and shook her head. 'But the bragging rights are pretty high, right?'

'I suppose. Look, if we're going to be playing for the same team, can I ask you something unrelated?'

'You can ask, but if it's personal I might not answer.'

'Have you ever heard of a guy called Scott Mulvaney?'

'Ah, so it's not personal,' she said. 'Is this to do with the case you're working on?'

'That's where his name came up.'

She thought for a moment. 'I can't say the name rings a bell. Why? What's he done?'

'He did time for something violent. He spent the last year of that sentence in Lockstock Open Prison.'

'When was this?'

'He would have been released from Lockstock about three years ago, give or take.'

'Okay, so why do you want to find him?'

'He told a guy he was offered fifty grand to kill a woman in a caravan.'

'And did he?'

'That's what I'm hoping to find out. Even if I could find out who offered the money, it might be a big help.'

'If this roast is as good as you say it is,' Robbins said, 'I might be persuaded to make some discreet inquiries.'

'It's a deal,' said Slater. 'Trust me — you won't be disappointed.'

CHAPTER NINETEEN

'We were right about her being taken off the case, then?' asked Norman when Slater told him about Robbins on Monday morning.

'Right on the money, which means you were almost certainly right about Watson being some sort of undercover spy.'

'So, how are we going to work both cases? Does this mean you're not going to be working the Steve Harris case?'

'I don't think it's going to come to that,' replied Slater. 'Robbins is going to have to be careful what she does, and I promised not to go dropping her in the crap by making lots of waves. I'm going to have to wait to see what she can uncover. It's going to be very much a case of softly, softly. It might even turn out that we don't get anywhere.

'And as for the Steve Harris case, I intend to be working with you just like we were before, and now we've got a contact in Winchester nick who might be able to help too.'

'So, what do you need me to do?'

'Help me make sense of anything we find. Is that okay?'

'Is that okay? Are you kidding? Look, someone dragged you into a murder case by using a copy of your car to kill a guy. I'll help in any way I can.'

'Thanks, Norm. I told Robbins we could count on you,' said Slater. 'And I think it's pretty obvious Watson is the "someone" in question.'

'It's difficult to see how she couldn't be involved, but unless we can prove different, I would think she was probably working to orders, so let's not rush to judge, huh?'

'It would be a bloody sight easier if she'd only talk to me,' said Slater.

'She's probably following orders about that, too.'

Slater sighed. 'Yeah, you're probably right.'

'So, Robbins is okay?' asked Norman.

'Yeah, she's alright.'

'She does understand the risk she's taking?'

'I tried to persuade her she needn't get involved, but she's had her nose put out of joint, and she wants to know who's responsible. She knows the risk — that's why she's going to be very careful and take her time.'

'And you think you can avoid getting carried away and landing her in trouble?'

'I'm a changed man, remember? I'm much better at thinking before I act.'

'Actually, I have to confess I was impressed with the way you handled that young DS Wesley. He was trying so hard to wind you up.'

Slater folded his arms. 'Well, there you go. That proves my point.'

'Remember: Robbins is sticking her neck out for you.'

'I know, Norm. Trust me, I'm going to be on my best behaviour.'

* * *

'There's a message on the answering machine,' said Norman as he opened the office door.

'That's something we need to figure out if we're going to move forward,' said Slater. 'I still think we need a receptionist or something.'

'Yeah, right,' said Norman, grumpily, as he headed for his desk. 'If you know someone who works for nothing, maybe you can put me in touch with them. In the meantime, we'll have to make do with the machine.'

Slater didn't think there was any need for Norm to get the hump but decided that if his friend felt like that, he would be better left to his own devices. He made his way through to their 'incident room' and opened his laptop.

It was Norman's habit to make a peace offering in the form of tea if he felt he had been unnecessarily tetchy. Sure enough, ten minutes later he wandered in carrying two steaming mugs.

'I've been trying to get hold of Eddie Smith,' he said.

Slater raised a questioning eyebrow.

'Eddie Smith,' Norman repeated, and then rolled his eyes. 'You remember, Steve Harris was having an affair with his wife, Jackie, the weekend Julie Harris was killed.'

'Ah, yes, him. Pretty nasty character from what we've heard about him so far, if I recall,' said Slater. 'Go on.'

'I've left messages for him at home and got nowhere, so before we came out this morning, I called his work and left a message. They just called back. Apparently, Smith has taken a week off to go to some football match in Spain. He's not due back at work until next Monday.'

Slater took the mug Norman offered. 'Yeah, that figures. I used my Sunday evening to look at the football connection. By some miracle, Newcastle are playing in Europe this year. I believe they're playing in Madrid on Tuesday night. He'll probably be back before the weekend.'

'That's a pity. I would have liked to see what he had to say about the bullying allegations.'

'It'll keep until he gets back. It's not as if he's gone on the run. He doesn't even know we're looking for him yet, and it just so happens I've already checked out a few facts without his input.'

'Like what?'

'Steve Harris said Smith liked his football and rarely missed a match. I thought it might be an idea to check out where Newcastle were playing on the weekend Julie died, so I did a search. It turns out that was an FA Cup weekend, and Newcastle were at home to Manchester United.'

'But according to the alibis, he was at home with Jackie all weekend.'

'Yeah, that's what they said,' said Slater, doubtfully, 'but I can't believe any self-respecting Newcastle United season ticket holder would have missed a game as big as that!'

'Maybe we can find one of his friends that Harris mentioned,' said Norman. 'Perhaps they can remember what happened that weekend.'

'Yeah, but don't be surprised if they're in Spain with our friend Eddie right now.'

'Crap! I hadn't thought of that,' said Norman.

'I'll give it a try, you never know, we might get lucky,' said Slater. 'Guys have been known to grow up and move on. Maybe, ten years on, one of the other guys has found something more important than football, like a wife and kids.'

'I guess we need to track them down anyway.'

'I'll do it next. What are you up to?'

'I know this priest who took the confession is supposed to be missing, but I'm going to see if I can find him,' said Norman. 'It would help if he could explain why Jackie Smith suddenly decided to confess.'

'Didn't Debbie say she wanted to clear her conscience before she died?'

'I'm not sure I buy that. Jackie had lived with the lie for years,' said Norman. 'Why tell the truth now? Why not take her secret with her?'

'If she was a devout Catholic, maybe she believed all that stuff about confessing and receiving absolution. Personally, I don't see why that should make everything alright, but then what do I know?'

Before Slater could answer, the telephone began ringing.

'I'll get that,' said Norman, 'I was going back to my desk anyway.'

As Norman left the room, Slater turned back to his laptop and opened up his web browser.

Two minutes later, Norman popped his smiling face around the door.

'Cancel tomorrow's trip to the beauty salon,' he said, 'you'll have to do as you are.'

'Where are we going?'

'Amy Pritchard, the widow of the dead partner at Pritchard and Harkness, has agreed to speak to us.'

CHAPTER TWENTY

Slater walked into the front office, where he found Norman hunched over his laptop. 'I found one of Eddie Smith's mates. It seems Kenny James has outgrown being a football fan. I thought we could go and see him this afternoon.'

'Yeah, why not?' said Norman. 'There's only so much online research a man can take.'

'I've also been taking another look at Pritchard and Harkness,' said Slater. 'They must be pretty good at what they do; they make shedloads of money.'

'That would explain the plush offices then,' said Norman, over his shoulder, 'and how Harkness can afford to keep his wife in such luxury.'

'She lives so well because she owns twenty-five percent of the company, as does Amy Pritchard.'

'And does Harkness own the rest?'

'Not quite. He owns forty percent,' said Slater.

'Who does own the rest?'

'I haven't found that out yet.'

'No wonder they all live so well.'

'Yeah, Harkness might be an arse, but he obviously knows how to run a successful business.'

Norman turned from his desk. 'You'll be pleased to know I finally tracked down the priest.'

'Great! Is he very far away?'

'Southampton.'

'Can we go and see him? We can be there in an hour.'

'Well, yes, we can go, but I don't think there's much point.'

Slater thought Norman should have been looking more pleased with himself. 'What do you mean there's not much point? He could be the star witness.'

'I don't think so.'

'Why not?'

'I think you'll find a star witness has to be alive to be believable.'

Oh, crap,' said Slater. 'Really? What happened?'

'According to the retirement home, he had a heart attack.'

'Anything suspicious about it?'

'No, I don't think so. The person I spoke to said he was never in the best of health. It was natural causes.'

'Dammit!' said Slater. 'If we could have persuaded him to make a statement, we might have made a good case for Harris's innocence.'

'You really don't think he did it, do you?'

'The guy's obviously no saint, but I'm not convinced he's capable of murder.'

Norman swivelled his chair from side to side as he thought. 'Okay,' he said after a few seconds. 'How about this? Let's assume the alibi is sound, and Steve was with Jackie Smith that weekend. In that case, the way I see it, the most damning piece of evidence against him is the witness who claims he saw the car.'

'You're right. And it was very convenient the way the guy remembered the number plate. I mean, do you recall the registration number of every car you see?'

'No way.'

'Exactly. If something happens, and then you see a suspicious car, you might recall it, but to recall it several weeks after the event? I'm not sure I buy that.'

Norman was sorting through the pile of evidence. 'I've got the guy's details here somewhere. Yep, here you go. His name is Rhodri Evans.'

'Rhodri? That's Welsh, isn't it?' asked Slater.

'Yeah, that's right,' said Norman reading through the file. 'Crap!'

'What's up?'

'We could have killed two birds with one stone when we went down to the caravan park.'

'Don't tell me, he lives near there, right?'

'Near? He was living on the site at the time of the murder. It says here he was one of the staff who was resident on site. I'm sorry, I should have noticed that before. We could have saved ourselves some time.'

'Don't blame yourself,' said Slater. 'There are two of us, don't forget. I didn't see it either.'

'To be fair, you do have other things going on to distract you,' said Norman.

'How about we agree we missed it, and we shouldn't have.'

Norman swivelled his chair and reached for the phone. 'I'll get hold of Ivor Jones and see if he knows where we can find the sharp-eyed Mr Evans.'

* * *

Fifteen minutes later, Norman joined Slater in front of their evidence wall. His partner was reading through one of the files. He looked up to acknowledge Norman but carried on reading as he listened.

'Rhodri doesn't work at the caravan park any more,' said Norman.

'Yeah, well, it would have been a bit too easy if he had been there waiting to talk to us, wouldn't it?' said Slater. 'Did they say where we could find him?'

'Apparently he bought himself a house in a small town called Llangwelli.'

'That caravan park must pay better than I thought.'

'No, I don't think so. Even Ivor Jones admits the pay's crap. He also said he was glad to see the back of Evans, who was so lazy he couldn't be relied on to do anything. In his opinion, the man will never amount to anything.'

'Well, he got that wrong if the guy's gone on to buy a house.'

'But he didn't get the house through hard work,' said Norman. 'He won a hundred grand.'

'Won it? On what?'

'He told them it was on the lottery.'

An expression of disbelief crossed Slater's face. 'Doesn't it piss you off when people like that win big? Think of all the people who work their nuts off and get little or no reward, and then a waster like that wins a fortune. It's not right.'

'I might be just a bit over-suspicious,' said Norman. 'But it may be even more "not right" than you think.'

Slater's head snapped up from his reading. 'Go on.'

'It turns out the big win happened just after Evans testified at Steve Harris's trial.'

'That's interesting.'

'You think?' said Norman. 'Then wait until you hear the next bit. According to Ivor Jones, Evans never mentioned to anyone at the caravan park that he'd seen the car. No one knew anything about it until he asked for time off to appear as a witness at the trial. And then, immediately after the trial, he quit his job. Doesn't that seem a bit strange to you?'

'From what we've heard so far, I would expect him to be the sort of guy who would brag about being a witness,' said Slater.

'That's how I see it too,' said Norman.

'What was the name of that town again?'

'Llangwelli. It's about twenty miles beyond the caravan park.'

'Well, now we've got my comfy car back, I suggest we use it to get there if that's okay?' said Slater.

'Do you really think I'm going to refuse to be chauffeur-driven each way after all the driving I've been doing?'

'When do you want to go?'

'We've got Amy Pritchard lined up for the morning.'

'Wednesday then?'

Norman pondered. 'Why don't we take a leisurely drive down tomorrow afternoon? I'm sure we can find a small hotel or a B & B, and then we'll get a full morning down there on Wednesday and be back by dinner time.'

'Would I be right in thinking you have a date on Wednesday night, but you don't have one on Tuesday?' teased Slater.

'I don't usually see them on Wednesday, but this week the kids have got something on at school and they want me to go and watch.'

'I'd better make sure I get you back home in time, then, hadn't I?'

CHAPTER TWENTY-ONE

Kenny James's workshop was tucked away in the corner of a small industrial estate. It was quite easy to find as there were several cars in varying states of disrepair crammed onto the tiny forecourt. Norman and Slater made their way through the roller door at the front of the building. In the background, an almost-tuned-in radio distorted a song so much as to make it unidentifiable.

'How the hell can anyone listen to that din, Norm?'

'Beats me. Maybe they have special hearing that distorts the distortion and converts it back into music.'

'I think I'd settle for earplugs.'

'I think I'd throw the radio in the bin,' said Norman, 'but that's because so much of this modern music sounds like crap whether it's distorted or not.'

'Can I help you guys?' called a voice.

They spun round to see a man sliding out from under a car on a trolley.

'We're looking for Kenny James,' Norman said.

'That's me,' said the man, as he climbed to his feet. 'What can I do for you? We can do servicing, repairs and bodywork.'

'Sorry,' said Norman. 'We're not here to have a car fixed. We'd like to ask you a few questions, if you can spare a few minutes.'

'Questions? About what?'

'Ten years ago, a man called Steve Harris was sent to prison for murdering his wife,' said Slater. 'Some new evidence has come to light that makes the verdict questionable, and we've been asked to investigate.'

James narrowed his eyes. 'You mean you're the police?'

'No, Mr James, we're not the police. We're private investigators working for the convicted man's sister.'

'I don't have to speak to you?'

'No, you don't have to speak to us.'

'So why should I?'

'Wouldn't you want to help a man who is in prison for something he didn't do?' asked Norman.

'Well, yeah, but what's any of this got to do with me?'

'Do you remember the case?'

James gave a hollow laugh. 'Blimey, everybody around here remembers the case. It's not every day someone who lives not half a mile from you gets murdered by their husband, is it?'

'Did you know Steve or Julie Harris?'

'I think I might have come across him in the pub once or twice, but I never really knew him.'

'How about a man called Eddie Smith, d'you know him?' asked Slater.

James's eyes narrowed again. 'Yeah, I know him. I used to be mates with him back then, but I don't see him these days. We used to go to football together, but I stopped doing that when I met my missus.'

'Some things are more important, right?' asked Norman.

'You grow up and your priorities change, don't they?'

'That must be an expensive pastime,' said Slater.

James smiled. 'What, having a wife? You're not kidding. That's why I needed to stop going to football and start working hard. It was worth it, though.'

'Can you remember anything about the time Julie Harris died?' asked Norman.

'I don't understand why you're asking me these questions. I told you, I hardly knew this Harris bloke, and I don't think I ever knew his wife. Anyway, wasn't she killed in some caravan place in Wales? I've never even been to Wales.'

'We wanted to know what you could tell us about Eddie Smith,' said Slater.

'Eddie? What do you want to know about him?'

'Like where he was the weekend Julie died.'

'You think Eddie killed her? Why would he do that?'

'Harris was a ladies' man. Eddie's wife was his sister-in-law. There's been a suggestion they may have been seeing each other.'

'And you think Eddie killed Harris's wife to get his own back? On a weekend during the football season? You must be joking.'

'Do I look like I'm joking?' asked Slater.

'No, I suppose you don't,' said James, 'but you obviously don't know anything about Eddie Smith. He wouldn't miss a football match if his house were burning down.'

'What about if his wife was spending the weekend with Harris?'

'He'd want revenge, alright, but he wouldn't miss the match. He'd sort the pair of them out when he got back.'

'The pair of them?' asked Slater. 'He wasn't averse to giving his wife a bit of a slap, then? That's what all you tough guys do, is it?'

James turned to face Slater. 'Hey, wait a minute. Don't you try to pin a label like that on me, mate. Just because I used to waste my time with a thug like Eddie Smith doesn't mean I'm one too. I'd rather die than hurt my wife.'

Slater put his hands up, palms facing James. 'Sorry, no offence intended. But you admit Smith is a thug?'

'Eddie was alright if you didn't cross him, but he had a real mean streak in him, and he was bloody unpredictable, you know? You could take the piss one day, and then make the same joke another day and find yourself pinned up against the wall.'

'We've got compelling evidence to suggest he used to beat his wife up. Do you know if it's true?'

'There was a rumour,' admitted James, reluctantly, 'but I never actually saw him hit her or saw her with bruises or anything like that.'

'But you think it could be true?' asked Norman.

'I know for a fact the man was a bully and a thug, so it wouldn't be a great surprise.'

'Can you recall the weekend in question?' asked Slater.

'It was how many years ago? Ten, did you say? Jesus, I can't remember that far back, but I can tell you for sure, if it was in the football season, we would have been at a game, no question.'

'How about if I said it was an FA Cup weekend?'

James thought for a moment. 'That was the year we played United, wasn't it? Yeah, I'm sure it was. We were there all weekend. Got there Friday afternoon and didn't leave until sometime on Monday.'

'You're sure?' asked Norman. 'And you're sure Eddie Smith was there?'

'How often do you get to play Manchester United, at home, in the FA Cup? I'm certain, and I'll tell you why. Eddie started a fight after the game, and we all got arrested. That was the last straw for me, and it was the last season I was a regular. By the next year I had discovered better things to do, you know?'

'What did Eddie think of that?'

'He didn't like it, but then I didn't give a damn what he thought.'

CHAPTER TWENTY-TWO

Amy Pritchard was a small, graceful woman with enough streaks of silver and grey in her hair to suggest she might be somewhat older than she first appeared.

'When we spoke on the telephone you said you'd like to ask me some questions about Julie Harris,' she said as she handed each of them a cup of tea.

'That's right,' said Norman. 'Some new evidence has been found, and we've been asked to investigate further.'

'New evidence?'

'I'm afraid we're not at liberty to say what that evidence is.'

'No, of course not,' said Mrs Pritchard. 'But I'm not sure how I can be of much help. My memory's not what it was, you see.'

'I understand Julie was your husband's secretary. I was wondering if you could tell us anything about her. It will help us get a better picture of her and her life.'

'She wasn't only my husband's secretary, she worked for James Harkness too. In fact, I understood she worked more for him than for John.'

'But wasn't it your husband who interviewed Julie and employed her initially?'

'I seem to recall there were always two interviews, one with John and one with James, then they'd compare notes, but, to be honest, I was never really a part of the business, so I couldn't say for sure who had employed her.'

'I thought you were a director?' said Slater.

'Well, yes, I am, but I don't have anything to do with the day-to-day running of the company.'

'You have shares, is that right?'

'Yes, I do. Lots of people have shares in companies. It's not unusual.'

'No, of course not,' said Slater.

'What about Julie herself?' asked Norman. 'Can you tell us anything about her?'

'I think I only met the poor girl once or twice at social events, so I hardly knew her. I think I liked her. I'm sure I would have remembered if I hadn't. I'm sorry, I'm not much help, am I?'

'Can you recall your husband ever talking about Julie, Mrs Pritchard?' asked Slater. 'Did he ever mention her having trouble at home or anything like that?'

Her eyes creased as a mischievous smile flitted across her face. 'Are you working your way around to asking about John and Julie at the caravan?' she asked, surprising Slater so much he almost sprayed tea everywhere.

'You didn't know?' she said, once the spluttering had ceased.

'Know what?' asked Norman.

'I take it you know about the caravan?'

Norman nodded.

'There was a nasty rumour going around at one time that my husband had arranged to meet Julie at the caravan on the weekend she died. It was complete rubbish, of course.'

Norman looked at Slater, but it seemed neither of them could think what to say.

'My husband was a good man, who made sure I never wanted for anything,' she continued, 'but he met me on the rebound. His heart always belonged to another woman. The thing is, it wasn't Julie Harris. He was smitten with Sandra Harkness.'

'Ah,' was all Norman could think to say.

'Oh, I knew I was always going to be second best,' she continued, wistfully. 'I knew that from the day I met him. Sandra had just chosen James over him, you see. She was their secretary at the time. I suppose she was what you might call attractive, if you like that sort of thing. I got the impression she used to play one against the other and had come between the two men so much the business almost fell apart as a result.'

'That can happen,' said Norman.

'Fortunately, James had the sense to take his prize and remove her from the business before it was too late. He may be an absolute genius when it comes to running the business, but James Harkness isn't a very pleasant man. He's very selfish, and rarely made decisions for John's benefit, but that was one occasion when he did.

'I met John shortly before James and Sandra married. He used to tell me he owed everything to me because I stopped him from falling apart, but John was a painfully honest man and could never tell me he loved me because he never did. He only ever loved her.'

Slater was surprised to find he was feeling slightly embarrassed by the turn this conversation had taken, and he could see Norman looked pretty uncomfortable too.

She saw the look on their faces. 'I'm sorry. I didn't intend to embarrass anyone. I suppose that's not really what you came to hear, is it?'

'Anything we can learn about that time could prove useful,' said Norman, hoping he didn't sound too insincere.

'How did this rumour about the caravan start?' asked Slater.

'Julie was responsible for keeping track of the bookings, not that they had many. It seemed the people who worked for them didn't find a caravan down by the coast as appealing as James had thought, so it was empty most of the time.'

'I'm sorry to interrupt,' said Slater, 'but did you say it was James Harkness's idea to buy the caravan?'

'Oh yes. John thought it was a waste of money, but he went along with it because he was a twitcher and he believed he would be able to use the caravan for birdwatching on some of the weekends it was empty. Because she looked after the bookings, Julie knew when it was empty, and she kept him informed. When her body was found there was some suggestion John was there that weekend too, but it wasn't true, he was actually in Scotland.'

'Did you go with him?' asked Slater.

'When my husband was birdwatching, I became invisible. I'd rather be invisible in my own surroundings than in some lodge up in Scotland.'

'Does that mean you were here?'

'Am I a suspect or something?'

'We're starting with a blank canvas, Mrs Pritchard,' said Slater. 'So, everyone's a suspect and no one's a suspect.'

She gave him a disapproving look.

'Did he go away every weekend?' asked Norman.

'Mostly,' she said, sadly. 'Sandra came first, then the wretched birds, and then me. I was an afterthought.'

'Err, I'm sorry to have to ask,' said Norman, 'but didn't your husband commit suicide?'

'Yes, he did,' she said. 'And yes, he did leave a note, saying how sorry he was and how he couldn't live with the guilt any longer.'

'Guilt?' asked Norman.

'Yes, guilt about the way he had treated me.' She made the statement as if it was an incontrovertible truth.

'Ah, right, I see,' said Norman, doubtfully.

There was the briefest of hesitations, and then she got to her feet. 'I found an old photo album I thought might be of use to you. The photos are taken from the year before Julie died. They include the firm's Christmas party, and the summer barbecue.'

She opened a drawer and handed the album to Norman, who carefully opened it and began to thumb his way through the photos.

'There's no delicate way of asking this,' said Slater, carefully, 'but do you think your husband could have been having an affair with Julie Harris? You did say he was away nearly every weekend.'

She gave Slater an indulgent smile. 'I obviously haven't made myself clear. I can assure you the only affair my poor husband would have been interested in would have been with Sandra Harkness, and I never had reason to think that had ever happened.'

'Do you think we might borrow this album, Mrs Pritchard?' asked Norman. 'There are one or two photos here that might be useful, and they will certainly help us put faces to names. We can copy the photos we need, and then we'll return it.'

'Of course. You can keep it for as long as you need it. I'm not sure I even want it back.'

* * *

'I have to say, I liked Amy Pritchard very much,' said Norman, as they drove away.

'There's a "but" in there, Norm,' said Slater. 'Is it the same "but" as mine?'

Norman sighed. 'I'm afraid she was just a little too insistent about her husband being some sort of saint, wasn't she?'

'And way too sure his guilty note was about his love for Sandra Harkness,' said Slater. 'It could as easily be guilt about Julie Harris.'

'Harkness hinted much the same,' said Norman.

'There was no love lost there, was there? She certainly doesn't like James Harkness.'

'Maybe he tried the old wandering hands thing with her.'

'Or maybe he knows something about her old man and Sandra that she would rather be kept quiet,' said Slater.

'Harkness also said it was John Pritchard's idea to buy the caravan. Now Pritchard's wife says it wasn't. Somebody's lying somewhere.'

There was a short silence while they thought about this.

'Are you going to tell me what you found in the photo album that made you want to keep it?' asked Slater.

'Well, it's funny you should mention liars. You remember James Harkness said he hardly knew Julie Harris?'

'What did you find?'

'There's a photograph of John and Amy Pritchard dancing together. Guess who's dancing up close and personal in the background?'

'Harkness and Julie Harris?'

'So close they're almost as one,' said Norman, 'and Sandra Harkness is right there too, looking daggers at the happy couple.'

'And so, the plot thickens,' said Slater. 'I had my doubts about Harkness when we met him, but now you've found the photograph I think we might have to reconsider every single word he said.'

'I'd love to know what Sandra Harkness had to say about this,' said Norman.

'So, why don't we go and ask her?'

'What, right now?'

'There's no time like the present.'

'But it's half an hour away, and we're supposed to going to Wales.'

'Don't worry, Wales will still be there. Why don't you call her now, and make sure she's at home. If she is, we'll do it now.'

CHAPTER TWENTY-THREE

Sandra Harkness lived in the sort of country house that would cost millions to buy. When she opened the door, Slater thought Sandra had hardly aged from the photographs in the album, and they had been taken twelve years ago. She was apparently used to the more elegant things in life, and the interior of the house looked like something straight out of a magazine.

'What was it you wanted to ask me about?' she said as she led them into a luxurious living room. 'I know you told me over the phone . . .'

'We're here to ask what you can tell us about Julie Harris, who used to work for your husband. She was murdered ten years ago,' said Norman.

'Ah, yes, that's right, I remember now. What is it you want to know?'

'Anything you can tell us will help.'

'I'm not sure I can remember her,' she said.

'Maybe this will jog your memory,' said Slater.

He handed her the photograph of James Harkness dancing with Julie Harris. Sandra took a quick look at the photo and then did a double take.

'I think that's you watching the dancers, isn't it? Remember her now?'

'Ah. Yes, I remember her.'

'We thought you might,' said Norman. 'What can you tell us about her?'

'She was trouble right from the start.'

'Oh, really? We were getting the impression she was well liked.'

'Well, I didn't like her. Coming into the office half-dressed. It's not the behaviour of a professional secretary. It's no wonder my husband and John Pritchard were drooling all over her.'

'Your husband told us he hardly knew Julie,' said Norman.

'Yes, well, he would, he's a liar.'

'So, you're saying he did know her, quite well?'

'No, I'm saying knew her very well.'

'We were getting the impression she wasn't like that.'

'You don't have to be "like that" with my husband. If he takes a shine to you, it's tough to say no. He's not averse to groping and pawing.'

'Is that what he did with you?' asked Slater.

'What does that mean?'

'Didn't you work there as a secretary? I understand you turned one or two heads back then. Surely a man like that would have had his hands all over you.'

'I would have slapped his face if he had,' she said, vehemently. 'When I first met him, he was a complete gentleman. It was after we married that he turned into an animal.'

'Why don't you divorce him?' asked Norman.

She looked around the room. 'And give up all this?'

'The money makes up for the groping? It must be hard to live with a man like that,' said Slater.

'I don't live with him. He lives in a flat close to the office in Winchester.'

'That must be an expensive way for a couple to live.'

'There's no shortage of money to pay for it, I can assure you. It works just fine for us, and it's not as if I'm a kept woman. I'm one of the company directors, and I'm a shareholder.'

She gave him a smile that suggested she was going to say no more on that particular subject.

'Okay, let's talk about something else, then,' said Slater. 'What can you tell us about John Pritchard?'

'What do you want to know?'

'Anything you can tell us. If you were the secretary when you met your husband, you must have known John.'

She smiled fondly. 'Poor John, he thought he had a chance with me.'

'Wasn't he married?'

'This was before he met Amy,' she said. 'He was delightful at first, very charming, but he became rather like a puppy following me around all the time. It was a pity, but he was much older than me anyway.'

'Isn't your husband older than you?'

'Not as much as John was. Besides, John was a bit soft. I wanted someone with a bit more about them.'

'You mean you dropped him and took up with his business partner instead.'

'Oh, get over yourself,' she said. 'People meet, they decide they're not right for each other, and they move on. It happens.'

'Do you think John Pritchard could have been having an affair with Julie Harris?' asked Slater.

'Good heavens, no!'

'You seem very sure about that,' said Norman.

'Who on earth told you that?'

'I heard there was a rumour he was with Julie the weekend she died.'

'He couldn't have been with her, he was . . .' She stopped mid-sentence.

'He was where, Mrs Harkness?' asked Norman.

She shifted awkwardly in her seat and licked her lips. 'Wasn't he in Scotland watching stupid birds or something?'

'You tell us,' said Slater.

'He was in Scotland, birdwatching.'

'At the lodge your company owns.'

'I'm sure Amy can tell you exactly where he was. She used to watch him like a hawk.'

'Now, why would she do that?'

'Because she thought he was seeing me. She always thought he was seeing me.'

'And was he?'

'I don't see what that has to do with Julie Harris getting murdered.'

'But if you could say with certainty where John Pritchard was, we could eliminate him from our enquiry. He can't speak for himself, you see, and there is this rumour . . .'

'Well, I'm sorry, I can't help you with that. As I said, Amy will know where John was.'

'And where were you that weekend?' asked Slater.

'I don't think that's any of your damned business!'

'This is a murder investigation.'

'I think you'll find the police conducted that investigation ten years ago, and a man was found guilty. I was never a suspect then, and I'm not one now, and you're not the police. If you must know, I was here with my husband.'

'Well, then, you have nothing to worry about,' said Slater.

'Can you tell us anything about the caravan owned by your husband's company?' asked Norman.

'If you mean that horrible little place in the back of beyond, I only ever went there once. It wasn't my cup of tea at all.'

'Can you recall whose idea it was to buy the caravan?'

'That would have been James,' she said, very definitely.

'You're sure about that? It couldn't have been John's idea?'

'John told me he only went along with it because he thought it would be a good place to do his twitching, or whatever it's called.'

'You mean birdwatching?'

'Yes, that's it.'

'You don't think he would have gone there for any other reason?'

'If you mean would he have taken a woman there, definitely not. John was the sort of man who would make sure a woman only had the best.'

* * *

'What did you make of that?' asked Norman as he drove away.

'She sure doesn't have much time for her husband.'

'Yeah, she didn't leave much room for doubt about that.'

'What about her and John Pritchard?' asked Slater.

'You mean you think there's only one way she could have been so sure how he would treat a woman if he took her away for a weekend?'

'You picked up on that, too? It's an intriguing possibility, but she could have found that out before she agreed to become Mrs Harkness, so it doesn't necessarily mean anything.'

'It will be interesting to see what Amy Pritchard has to say about Sandra and John,' said Norman.

'What do you think she was going to say when she hesitated about John Pritchard being in Scotland?'

'Yeah, that was weird, wasn't it?' agreed Slater. 'Maybe she knows something we should know.'

'D'you think it's worth coming back again?'

'I think we made it clear John Pritchard is a suspect who can't defend himself. Let's give her a few days to think about it. If we're making no progress by then, it might be worth coming back to try again.'

CHAPTER TWENTY-FOUR

As planned, Slater and Norman took a leisurely drive down to Wales later that afternoon. When they finally reached their destination just before seven p.m., Slater's first thought was that whoever had decided Llangwelli should be designated a small town apparently had no idea what a village was.

'That must be the smallest town I ever saw,' said Norman, as they passed a handful of houses and were suddenly back on the open road.

'We can't be through it already,' said Slater. 'There were only about twenty houses.'

'Maybe this main road cuts past the edge of town. Perhaps if we had turned left back there, as I suggested, we would have gone into the actual town and not just past the outskirts.'

'Okay, smartarse,' said Slater. 'I'll turn around and we can try your way.'

He soon found a suitable spot, turned the car around, and headed back the way they had come, turning off the main road as Norman had suggested.

'There you go,' said Norman. 'It's almost a metropolis.'

'Only if two small shops and a pub counts as a metropolis.'

'Someone obviously thought that was enough to make a town, so why not?'

There was a small square with three or four tiny shops and one large pub. A sign hanging outside the pub saying *B & B* suggested they may well have found their destination. Half an hour later they had booked in, taken their cases up to their rooms, and were back down in the bar.

As they studied the not-very-extensive menu, the landlord pulled two pints for them. 'So, what brings you two gents to Llangwelli?'

'We're looking for a guy called Rhodri Evans,' said Norman.

The man pulled a face. 'What's that idiot done now?'

'Do you know him?' asked Norman.

'Everybody in this town knows him. He's like chewing gum on your shoe, bloody hard to get rid of.'

'Do you know where we can find him?'

'What are you, debt collectors?'

'Would that be a problem?' asked Slater.

'Not for me, but the last time he had debt collectors after him they found him in here and there was a fight. I don't need trouble like that.'

'Do we look like troublemakers?'

'The last lot didn't look like it until it all kicked off.'

'Trust me, we're not looking to pick a fight with anyone,' said Norman. 'We're investigating a murder that happened ten years ago. Rhodri was a witness at the trial. All we want to do is ask him a few questions and check his story.'

The landlord didn't look convinced.

'Does he come in here?' asked Slater.

'More often than I like.'

'Will he be in here tonight?'

'Maybe later. Are you going to ambush him in here? I just told you I don't want a fight in my bar.'

'As a gesture of goodwill, how about we eat our dinners and then go to our rooms?' said Norman. 'That will make sure there's no fight, and then if you tell us where he lives at breakfast in the morning, we'll go and speak to him there.'

'I promise we're not looking to cause trouble for anyone,' said Slater. 'Once we've spoken to him, we'll be gone.'

CHAPTER TWENTY-FIVE

Slater wasn't best pleased to find himself back in his room before eight p.m., but as Norman had pointed out, it meant they would find out where Rhodri Evans lived. They could speak to him first thing tomorrow and be on their way home before lunchtime.

He switched on the tiny TV and tried to find something worth watching, but, as so often happened, there was nothing that appealed to him. Then his mobile phone started to ring, and he forgot about the TV.

'Hi, it's Robbins.'

'I thought you were going to keep a low profile,' said Slater. 'You can't be doing that if you've got more info already. I didn't expect to hear from you again for days. I really think you should back off a bit. You're taking a lot of risks.'

'I admit, I've had to be even more careful than I thought I would. It seems my boss thinks I might be tempted to take matters into my own hands. I can't imagine where he got that idea.'

'It sounds to me like he knows you well. Or maybe he had his nose put out of joint too, and he's tempted himself.'

'Well, whatever, here's what I've got so far. First off, I wanted to see if we could find out who drove that car the night Lenkov died. My God, it's taken hours, but I got it eventually. They made sure we couldn't use CCTV from the immediate area, but we've got footage from further out, and it clearly shows a car bearing your number plates being driven into Winchester the night Lenkov died, and better still, we've got one that shows the driver.'

'Can you see who it is?'

'Whoever it was they're wearing a baseball cap pulled down low over their face, but I'm pretty sure I can see some long blonde hair hanging out of the cap.'

'You think it's Samantha Brearley?'

'I couldn't say for certain, but it's possible.'

'Bloody hell, d'you think she detonated the bomb?'

'I don't think we'll ever know that for sure,' said Robbins. 'There could be a whole team of people already on site waiting for her to lure Lenkov into position.'

'What else have you got?'

'Those parking tickets on your car are fake.'

'Are you sure? Why would anyone fake them?'

'I got them checked out by the company that runs the station car park, and by the local council. They don't have the right serial numbers. They're definitely fake tickets. As to why they used fakes? To throw you off the scent and make it look as though your car had been there all week.'

'Do you think the car might have only arrived there the morning it was found?'

'I don't think it did, I'm certain it did. The car park CCTV stopped working sometime after two o'clock on Sunday morning. At least that's the last recorded footage.'

'That's convenient,' said Slater.

'Isn't it just? It's the only time it wasn't working during the whole week. My bet is the car must have been parked there during the early hours of Sunday morning.'

'And they knocked out the CCTV, so we've got no way of knowing who dumped it there.'

'Unless that person used a train to get away. We've got a possible suspect.'

'You're quite good at this, aren't you?' said Slater.

'I didn't get to be detective inspector because I was a moron.'

'Don't tell me, your suspect was wearing a baseball cap, and you can't see her face.'

'It's worse than that. Whoever it is, they're hiding behind an umbrella, but there's no doubt it's a woman. We have no way of proving she got out of your car — all we know is she got onto the train. But she didn't walk to the station from the town, so she must have come from the car park.'

'Could it be Watson?'

'Well, yes, it could be, but then it could as easily be me,' said Robbins. 'If it is her, she certainly knows how to keep her face hidden from the cameras.'

'What about the train? Is there any CCTV in the carriage she was using?'

'Oh sure, but she keeps the umbrella up until she's down in the seat. We never get a clear shot of her.'

'Bugger,' said Slater.

'Yes, it certainly is,' agreed Robbins.

'You've made a lot of progress.'

'I'm not so sure I have. Okay, so we know when these events happened, but we've got no proof who's behind them. They've left us a few hints but taken away enough to make sure we can't prove anything. All we have are our suspicions.'

'I think you should let it drop, at least for a week or so,' said Slater. 'If they've left hints, it could be they're tracking those hints to see if anyone comes looking for them. You could be walking into a trap.'

'D'you think so?'

'These people are experts in being devious, aren't they? They certainly don't care about what we might call right and wrong, and they wouldn't think twice about ending a career if it suited them.'

'My boss is a good bloke. He's got my back.'

'I don't doubt that for one minute, but I'll bet they'd be quite happy to shoot him down in flames as well.'

'Maybe you're right,' she said, gloomily. 'Okay, I'll leave it be for a few days, but I'm not giving up.'

'I didn't say give it up; I said be careful. In the meantime, I'll see if I can learn anything my end. I'll let you know if I find anything.'

CHAPTER TWENTY-SIX

Just after nine a.m. on Wednesday morning, Slater drove into the road where Rhodri Evans lived.

'The landlord was right when he said you wouldn't be able to miss the house,' he said.

'Sheesh, I thought he must have been exaggerating,' said Norman.

'Well, there you have it,' said Slater. 'Grass a foot long and crap everywhere, just like he said. It's a pity when the rest of the estate is so neat and tidy.'

'Yeah, his neighbours must love him,' said Norman.

Slater parked the car a short distance along from the house, and they both stared at it for a few moments.

'It must have been quite nice when it was built,' said Slater.

'Yeah, it's a pity no one has thought to clean the windows in the ten years since.'

'I suppose it saves on curtains.'

'Maybe he thinks if he can't see all the rubbish piling up outside he can pretend it's not his,' said Norman.

'D'you think he cares?'

Norman turned to look at Slater. 'About the rubbish? Or what the neighbours think? I think you'll find guys like this don't give a damn either way.'

Slater sighed. He didn't feel like dealing with a slob this morning. 'I suppose as we've come all this way to speak to the guy we'd better get on with it.'

'Don't forget I have a date tonight,' said Norman. 'So yes, let's go. The sooner we do it, the sooner we can go back home.'

They climbed from the car and carefully picked their way through the assorted rubbish. To their surprise, there was a bell attached to the front door, but when Norman pressed it, they couldn't hear it ringing inside. When he let go, the button popped out and dangled uselessly on the end of its spring.

'Ding bloody dong,' said Slater, wearily. He stepped forward, hammered on the door, and then waited, but there was no sign of life from inside. Then Norman tried pummelling the door, but still nothing happened. He stepped back and looked up at the upstairs windows.

'You don't think you're going to see anything through them, do you?' asked Slater.

Norman grinned at him. 'You're right,' he said, 'there's no chance, is there?'

He picked up an abandoned plastic shopping bag and walked over to the front window. He scrubbed at the window until he revealed a clean spot. His put his eye to the clean patch and then swore.

'What's up?' asked Slater.

'There's even more crap on the inside. I could clean the entire outside of this window and we still wouldn't see a single thing inside.'

'If this were a normal house I'd be surprised,' said Slater, 'but somehow, I'm not, I can't imagine why. I tell you what — you keep hammering on this door. I'm going to try around the back.'

Norman watched as Slater gingerly picked his way across to the side of the house and disappeared around the corner, then he began hammering on the door again.

Slater made his way down the side of the house until he came to a rickety gate. As a precaution, born of old habits, he slipped on a pair of latex gloves and then, careful not to make any more noise than he had to, he eased the latch and gently leaned against the gate. Unsurprisingly, it caught on the ground almost straight away, so Slater put his foot against the base and added a bit of shoulder higher up. To his dismay, the gate didn't swing open as he had hoped but just collapsed before him.

'Oh, bugger,' he muttered, as the gate crashed to the ground, taking him with it.

'Are you okay?' called Norman, peering around the corner of the house.

'The sodding gate collapsed,' said Slater, struggling back to his feet and brushing his jeans down.

Now Norman was grinning. 'You realise he would have to be deaf not to have heard all that noise.'

'If he hasn't heard us hammering on that front door, I'm pretty sure he won't have heard the gate, but you'd better keep an eye on that front door in case he tries to do a runner when I go in the back.'

As Norman disappeared back around the corner of the house, Slater was sure he heard him laughing, and he couldn't help but smile, too. It was getting to be like the old days, and he was beginning to enjoy himself.

He crept down the side of the house and peered around the corner. A wheelie bin overflowing with rubbish was off to one side, and assorted garden chairs in various states of disrepair were piled in a corner, but otherwise, the rubbish round this side was nowhere near as bad as he had expected.

He stopped at the kitchen window and tried to look inside, but it was like staring into a thick fog. He wiped a small patch in the dirty glass, but, just like with the windows at the front, it made no difference. Norman had been correct: there was even more crap on the inside.

He crept across to the kitchen door and gently tried the handle. It wasn't locked, so he eased the door open a couple of inches then waited a few seconds and listened hard. The only sound he could hear was the tick, tock, tick, tock of a clock, so he eased the door open enough to slip through into the kitchen.

Slater had been inside the house just a few seconds when he realised it was inordinately hot in there. 'Bloody hell,' he muttered. 'It's like an oven in here!'

Then he noticed something rather unpleasant, and this time he spoke more loudly. 'Oh, Jesus, what's that stink?'

He seemed to recall reading somewhere that every house has its own aroma, if only people had a keen enough sense of smell to detect it. It didn't need a bloodhound to find this one, and for a few nasty moments, Slater was sure he was going to be reacquainted with his breakfast.

Having satisfied himself his stomach wasn't going to embarrass him, and as there was apparently no one in, or at least awake, he made his way through to the front door and opened it to allow Norman to join him.

'Come on in,' he said. 'I don't think there's anyone here. But you should put some gloves on. It's impossible to know what you might be touching in here.'

'Is it that bad?' asked Norman as he made his way through the door. He stepped inside and then stopped in his tracks.

'It's a bit hot in here, isn't it?' he asked. Then: 'Holy Jesus, what the hell's that stink?'

'That's funny, that's more or less what I said.'

'That is not funny,' said Norman. 'It's disgusting. Have you any idea what it is?'

'I think the underlying odour is that of stale marijuana smoke. Then there's a frisson of rotten food from the kitchen sink, where the remains of a pizza are growing a rather stylish fur coat. There's also something else that I feel I should know, but I can't quite put my finger on right now.'

'Keeping the house at this temperature is an ideal way of encouraging everything to fester,' said Norman. 'Thank God it's not summer or it would be even worse, and there would be flies everywhere as well. How can people live like this?'

'It takes a special breed, that's for sure,' said Slater.

'I take it there's no sign of Evans?'

'Not down here but be my guest if you want to go upstairs and have a look around.'

'You're kidding, right? D'you really think he could have slept through all that noise?'

'Norm, if he smokes as much dope as I think he does, he could be comatose up there, and a bomb wouldn't wake him.'

'Do you really want me to check?'

'He's probably not here at all, but as we've come all this way to talk to him, we might as well make sure before we go back home.'

Norman began muttering to himself as he made his way to the stairs. He stopped at the bottom and looked up into the darkness. 'The windows are so shitty up there,' he said. 'It's almost like it's still night.'

'Try that switch thing on the wall,' said Slater. 'I think you'll find if you push it down, the lights come on.'

Norman glared at Slater, who looked back at him impassively.

'I didn't complain about you laughing when I fell over the gate,' said Slater, 'because I knew that if I bided my time, my chance would come, and sure enough, here I am getting my own back.'

Norman didn't have an answer to that, so he switched on the lights and started up the stairs.

'I'll have a nose around down here,' said Slater.

There was a small dining room off the kitchen. In the centre was a table, littered with papers. Slater made his way over and sifted through them. One of the items was a bank statement, and he found his eyes drawn to it.

He tutted as he read it. Then he saw something that made him draw his breath in sharply through his teeth.

'Well, well, Rhodri,' he said, quietly. 'What's this all about?'

There was what looked like a regular payment of £3,000 a month into his bank account, and yet he was overdrawn. Slater could see that nearly all of the withdrawals were in cash, but that didn't surprise him. After all, who pays their drug dealer by direct debit?

His thoughts were interrupted by the sound of Norman coming back down the stairs.

'Dave? You know you said there was a smell you should know, but couldn't identify? Well, we'd better call the police.'

As Slater began speaking, his brain was still connecting the dots. 'Why? What's up? Oh, crap. Is there a body up there?'

'You got it in one. I'm not sure if it's Evans, but whoever it is, we're too late to save him.'

'We could do without a complication like that. Has the body been dead long?'

Norman had his mobile phone in his hand and was tapping 999 into it. 'He's pretty ripe, so if I had to guess I'd say a few days, and possibly as much as a week, but then the heat in here would speed things up so I really can't be sure. I could be miles out.'

'So, it could have been much less?' asked Slater, thoughtfully.

'Yeah, could be,' agreed Norman, then, into his phone said, 'Hello? Yes, police, please.'

Slater had no desire to see the body upstairs, but there was something he did want to see. He thought he would probably find it in the hall, so he quickly checked and then went back to sifting through the stuff on the table.

'They'll be here in about twenty minutes,' said Norman, a couple of minutes later.

Slater handed Norman the bank statement he had found earlier. 'Here, take a look at this.'

Norman studied the statement and then looked up at Slater. 'Are you going to tell them about this when they get here?'

'What would you do?'

'Are there any more like this?'

'Two, or three.'

'Then they won't miss this one, will they?' He handed the statement back to Slater, who folded it small enough to slip into the back pocket of his jeans. 'They're going to want to know what we were doing here.'

'So, we'll tell them the truth,' Slater said.

'But we broke in.'

'The door was unlocked. I thought I smelled gas.'

'Are you kidding?'

'You can't deny it smells in here,' said Slater. 'Can I help it if I don't know what Welsh gas smells like?'

'Seriously?'

'Look, I almost got charged with murder last week. I don't want to have to go through all that again this week.'

'No one's going to accuse you of murder. Any fool can see we didn't murder the guy,' said Norman. 'But I don't think trying to be clever with the police is a good move for an adult to make, especially an adult who supposedly doesn't want any trouble.'

Slater thought about this for a moment. 'Okay, you're right, it's a stupid idea.'

'I suggest we tell them most of the truth,' said Norman. 'We can even show them there's a link with our case. With any luck, they'll be grateful for some leads, and we won't have to hang around too long.'

CHAPTER TWENTY-SEVEN

Detective Inspector Steffan Williams had been studying Slater and Norman for a good minute before he spoke. 'You're telling me you came all the way down here to speak with the dead man because you think he had been paid to lie at a trial ten years ago, is that right?'

Slater wondered how many more times they were going to have to explain, but he had promised Norman he would behave and not argue with anyone, and so far, he'd kept his word.

'That's it,' said Norman.

'I'm not a big fan of amateurs making their enquiries on my patch,' said Williams.

'I get that, but as we said before, we have over forty years' police experience between us, so we're not exactly beginners.'

Williams turned his gaze on Slater. 'And you say you're a detective inspector, have I got that right?'

'No, I said I was a DI until recently, but I quit,' said Slater, patiently.

'You're an uncooperative bugger, aren't you? Is there any particular reason you don't want to help us? Perhaps you think because we're in Wales we're all too thick to know our arse from our elbow, is that it?'

‘Actually, no, I don’t think you’re all stupid,’ said Slater. ‘But I’ve already explained what happened before and—’

‘You mean when your car got blown up and someone got killed, and you were a murder suspect, only it wasn’t your car, so now you’re not a suspect?’

‘Fine, if you want to put it like that,’ said Slater. ‘But do you think that’s the right attitude to make me warm to you, and want to help?’

Norman looked at his watch. The longer they were here, the less chance he had of being back on time, and the more chance there was of Slater losing his temper. ‘Can I make a suggestion?’ he asked.

Williams directed his gaze back in Norman’s direction. ‘Will it allow us to make some progress?’

‘I think so.’

‘Then please, proceed.’

‘You have a murder victim inside that house, and like any DI worth their salt, you want to find out who killed him, right?’

‘If you’re going to state the obvious, that’s hardly going to help, is it?’ said Williams.

‘It might if you’ll just let me finish,’ said Norman.

Williams nodded.

‘Okay, the first thing I want to point out is that if we hadn’t come here today, this guy could have been decomposing for weeks before anyone noticed. By that time, the body would probably have burst and been all over the shop. Any evidence would have been that much older, and harder, to find, right?’

Williams nodded again. ‘That’s true enough.’

‘So, we’ve done you a favour, right?’

Williams’ nod wasn’t quite so firm this time. ‘I’m not sure I’d agree you’ve done me a favour, but I get your point.’

‘Okay,’ continued Norman. ‘I’m assuming you don’t have us down as your prime suspects, am I right?’

‘Why would you think that?’

‘D’you want a list?’ asked Norman. ‘How about a) we wouldn’t have called the police, b) he’s been dead for days and we've only just arrived, c) we have witnesses who can prove we had no idea where the guy lived before last night. I could go on, but I think you get the point.'

Williams stared at Norman, and the slightest of smiles teased at the corners of his mouth. 'I'm going to need to know where you were last night, and when the pathologist figures out when the man died, I'll need to know where you were at the time.'

'Of course,' said Norman. 'That's no problem. The thing is, we think we might be able to help you, but so far none of your guys have been willing to listen to what we have to say. It's not that we don't want to help.'

'Okay,' said Williams, 'I'm listening now.'

'We've been digging around in this old case where a woman was murdered on a caravan site not far from here. We're becoming quite convinced the guy who was convicted was innocent. The dead guy here, Rhodri Evans, was the next person we wanted to speak to because it was his statement that sealed the conviction.'

'But why are you so sure he was lying?'

'Because just a short while after the trial, Rhodri was able to buy himself this house. He claims to have won a hundred grand on the lottery, but we checked. He never did.'

'We believe he was paid for his testimony,' added Slater. 'On Monday afternoon, we made a phone call to try and find out where he was, and three days later we find him dead. I know you'll find it for yourself, but I checked the central heating thermostat in the house. It was turned up as high as it would go, and the timer had been over-ridden, so it was on all the time. I wouldn't mind betting when your pathologist adds that into his calculations he'll suggest death occurred on Monday night.'

Williams stared from Norman to Slater and back to Norman. 'You think whoever you spoke to on Monday killed him?'

'You're a DI,' said Slater. 'Do you believe in coincidences?'

'We're not saying it's a cert,' said Norman, 'but don't you think it might be a good place to start?'

'One minute you don't want to help, and now you give me a prime suspect? Why should I believe you?'

'Have you got any better leads?' asked Norman.

'But what's in it for you?'

'Why does there have to be something in it for us?' asked Norman. 'We already told you we used to do what you do. We know how hard it can be. Why shouldn't we want to help just for the sake of it?'

Williams wasn't one for instant decisions, and now he thought for a minute. 'Have you made statements?'

'To three different officers,' said Slater, 'and we've given you our details, and I've told you about DI Robbins in Winchester. Give her a ring. She'll vouch for us.'

Williams fished the card Slater had given him from his pocket and studied it as if he thought it would tell him what to do.

'I tell you what I'll do,' he said. 'I'll give this DI Robbins a ring.'

He didn't notice Slater rolling his eyes as he keyed in the phone number. He took a few paces away, so they couldn't eavesdrop on his conversation, and Slater and Norman lowered their voices so Williams couldn't hear them.

'He likes to think about things, doesn't he?' said Slater.

'It's better than jumping to conclusions.'

'Yeah, I suppose so.'

'He seems to have a lot of respect around here,' said Norman. 'Everyone defers to him.'

'Or maybe he's just a complete arsehole and they're all scared of him.'

'You're just pissed off because he didn't go much on your hard luck story.' Norman knew he'd hit the target when Slater didn't respond, so he decided to rub it in just a bit. 'To be honest,' he went on, 'even I find it hard to believe the way you tell it, and I was there.'

'Hey, look, whose side are you on? There's still plenty of time for me to throw my toys out of the pram and make you late for your date.'

'You wouldn't do that,' said Norman confidently, but the look Slater gave him was enough to cause doubt.

Williams finished his call and turned back to them. 'I've spoken to DI Robbins, and she has more or less backed up your story.'

'What do you mean "more or less"?' asked Slater.

'That's for me to know,' said Williams, with a sly grin. 'DI Robbins has also agreed to be responsible for you should I need to speak to you again. And should I need to bring you into custody, she will arrange your arrests.'

'Arrests?' asked Norman.

They couldn't tell if Williams' smile was sincere or not.

'It's just a formality. I don't think it will be necessary, do you?'

CHAPTER TWENTY-EIGHT

It was after two thirty p.m. by the time Williams finally released them, and Slater was now trying to make good on the promise he had made to Norman about getting him home by seven o'clock.

'We're making a good time,' he said as they crossed the Severn Bridge back into England. 'As long as we don't hit any major holdups, we should be back by six thirty.'

'I have all my fingers crossed, and more,' said Norman.

'I'll get you there in time, trust me.'

'I'm beginning to think fate's working against us on this case, you know.'

'How d'you mean?'

'We had four potential witnesses — Jackie Smith, John Pritchard, the priest and now Rhodri Evans — who could have introduced one hell of a lot of doubt about the conviction, and they're all dead. It's like someone's working against us.'

'I have to admit, I was hoping we would find Eddie Smith wasn't at that football match. There's a good chance we wouldn't have needed any witnesses if that had been the case.'

'Yeah, out of the two of them, he probably deserves to serve time much more than Steve Harris. But having none of those witnesses is going to make it a bit difficult for us to prove Steve is innocent, don't you think?'

'It makes it more difficult, but not impossible,' said Slater. 'We'll just have to do it the hard way, and instead of proving Steve is innocent, we'll have to prove someone else is guilty.'

'You think we can do that?'

'I'm becoming increasingly convinced there's much more to this than first meets the eye. Take Rhodri Evans; I know we can't be sure yet, but I'd be prepared to bet a lot of money he died on Monday night.'

'You think Ivor Jones killed him?'

'Maybe not personally, but I'm sure he knows who did. It's too much of a coincidence that you call about Rhodri in the morning, and then he dies the same night.'

'If Ivor isn't the killer, it suggests there must be more than one person involved in this,' said Norman. 'Or do you think he's on his own, and he was the guy Julie was going to meet?'

'I don't think so, Norm. We've got no evidence to suggest anything like that, and anyway, he doesn't look capable.'

'Yeah, I can't argue with you on that.'

'But what about the bank statements I found?' said Slater. 'Can you think of any reason why someone would be paying a guy like Rhodri Evans three grand a month?'

'You mean apart from blackmail?'

'It has to be, doesn't it? But who's he blackmailing, and for what?'

'Well, he did stand up in court and say he'd seen Steve Harris's car. Maybe he thought a lump sum wasn't enough and he asked for monthly instalments as well.'

'Yeah, I've been thinking about that,' said Slater. 'A hundred grand is a lot to pay someone for lying in court.'

'You think he was paid to kill Julie Harris?' asked Norman.

'Don't you?'

'I guess it has to be a possibility.'

'You don't sound convinced,' said Slater.

'Well, I suppose it makes sense,' said Norman, 'but we've still got to figure out who paid him. Have you got someone in mind?'

‘How about Sandra Harkness? Don’t forget — she was the company secretary once, and James married her. Maybe she thought Julie Harris was getting too close to her husband and it was going to happen all over again, only this time she would be the loser. She openly admitted she likes her life of luxury, didn’t she?’

Norman was thinking. ‘Rhodri takes the hundred grand, murders Julie, and Sandra thinks that’s the end of it. But then Rhodri realises Sandra could be the cash cow that can keep him supplied with drugs for the rest of his life and starts blackmailing her.’

‘It adds up, doesn’t it?’

‘Only if we can get hold of her bank statement and prove she’s paying him every month. And then we’d still have to prove she paid him the big one.’

They drove on in silence for a few minutes, and then Norman spoke again. ‘Are you sure fate’s not working against us?’

‘Too many have died for it to be fate, Norm. I think someone has slowly, and carefully, been eliminating all the key witnesses who could prove Steve is innocent.’

‘Someone must really hate the poor guy.’

‘Or someone is being protected by keeping him inside. I think it’s time we narrowed down our suspects.’

‘I think it’s time we find out who owns that bank account,’ said Norman.

‘There’s no denying that would be handy, Norm, but we don’t have access to resources like that.’

‘You’re forgetting Vinnie,’ said Norman. Vinnie was Norman’s tame hacker. At least, that’s what Slater called him. Slater and Vinnie didn’t get on. ‘I know you don’t like him—’

‘He’s a hacker, and an arrogant git.’

Norman sighed. They had been through this particular argument many times before. ‘If you say so, but he’s also a genius. If I give him that bank account information, I guarantee we’ll know exactly whose it is by the morning.’

Slater didn't like the idea of being beholden to someone like Vinnie. Then again, what other way did they have of finding out what they needed to know?

'They won't be able to use it in court,' he said.

'So, we'll have to make sure they don't need to rely on it in court.'

'How are we going to do that?'

'I have no idea,' said Norman, 'but without it, we're probably going to be unable to prove anything.'

Slater knew Norman was right. 'Alright,' he said reluctantly. 'But I don't want to hear him gloating about how bloody amazing he is and how he's a genius and all that crap, okay?'

'Scout's honour,' said Norman. 'I'll speak to him later.'

CHAPTER TWENTY-NINE

At eight thirty that evening, Slater's mobile phone started ringing. He picked it up and checked the caller ID. It was Robbins.

'I had a call from a DI Williams this afternoon,' she said. 'We had an interesting chat about two amateur detectives who had messed up his crime scene. Apparently, you broke into a house and discovered a dead body. He wanted to know if he should have arrested you for murder.'

'We did not mess up his crime scene, and we did not break in. The door was unlocked. We didn't even know it was a crime scene until we got in there, and if we hadn't found the body, it could have lain there for weeks. We did him a favour. Anyway, what did you tell him?'

'I said I had asked myself exactly the same question about you a few days ago, and that if he'd made the wrong decision then so had I, and if that was the case, the chances are the two of you are serial killers.'

'What did he say to that?'

'He laughed.'

'Really? You made him laugh? We got the impression he'd had a sense of humour bypass.'

'The man was hoping for a few days' leave and then you two discover a body. Trust me, I wouldn't have found it funny either.'

'Now I understand why he was so pissed off. I suppose I've been there enough times,' said Slater. 'Tell him I'm sorry, next time you speak to him.'

'That's not the only reason I'm calling,' said Robbins. 'I thought it might be worth having a look at the CCTV cameras around the car parks at Gatwick on the night you came back from Thailand.'

'How does that help? We already know Watson took my car home that night,' said Slater.

'Yes, we do, but now we also know our friend Lenkov came out of the car park at the same time and followed her all the way out of the airport and onto the M23 motorway.'

'He followed her all the way to London?'

'I have a friend in Traffic. She has other friends in other traffic centres. We have both cars tracked, on ANPR, driving all the way up to, and into, London, and he's never very far behind her. It would be an amazing coincidence if he wasn't following her.'

'So that photograph wasn't doctored. He was in the airport lounge, but he was following Watson and not me. Somehow, he knew she was in Thailand with me, and my photograph led him to her.'

'My guess is he knew she was out there, and he must have had some idea when she was coming back, but he didn't know what the man she was with looked like, and that's why he had your photo on his phone. It meant he had two faces to look for instead of one. I bet he was hanging around the airport terminal all day, checking every flight back to the UK until he found her.'

'And I suppose if he had my photo and got stopped, anyone would think he was looking for me, and not her.'

'It certainly muddied the waters for our investigation, didn't it?'

'Do you think she knew he had followed her?' asked Slater.

'If she was working for who we think, and she worked undercover, she would have been trained in all this surveillance stuff. I'm sure she would have known.'

'If he followed her, he would have known my registration number. Do you think they drove the decoy car down knowing he would follow?'

'I think that's a perfectly reasonable assumption,' said Robbins. 'But I can't figure out why they came all the way down to Winchester. If it was a trap, why not do it in London?'

'Why blow the bloke up?' asked Slater. 'Why not just take him alive?'

'Ah, now you're getting into territory mere mortals like us aren't clever enough to understand. That's why they take all our evidence away and stop us investigating further.'

'That rankles a bit, doesn't it?'

'No,' she said, 'it rankles a lot, and irritates the hell out of me. I don't think it's right they can go around murdering people at will and then hide all the evidence, so we can't prove what happened.'

'Isn't that what they call "for the greater good"?'

'Greater good, my arse,' she said. 'If we went around killing people we believed were crooks, there would be a public outcry! We can't get away with it, so why should they?'

'You want to be careful,' said Slater. 'That's the sort of passionate stuff that gets you into hot water with the powers that be.'

'If that's the case, then so be it,' she said, vehemently. 'I can't be someone I'm not.'

'Hey, you're preaching to the converted here. I am on your side. I'm just saying be careful, that's all.'

He listened to Robbins' breathing over the phone, and he wondered if that was going to be the end of the conversation or if she had anything else to say.

'You asked me if I had ever heard of a guy called Scott Mulvaney,' she said.

Slater had almost forgotten about that. 'Yes, but there's no need to worry, we'll find him eventually.'

'No, you won't.'

'You seem very sure about that. What do you know that I don't?'

'People like Scott Mulvaney are easy to find on the police database because they have extensive records. In this case, violent crime was his speciality, so there were all sorts of markers against his name, making him easy to find.'

'I suppose he's inside again, is he?'

'The Scott Mulvaneys of this world are habitual criminals, so it was only a matter of time before he got involved in more violence. In his case, it took six months, only this time he was the victim, not the perpetrator.'

'You're telling me someone bumped him off, right?'

'I can see why you made it all the way to DI,' she said.

'Crap,' said Slater. 'That's another potential witness down the drain.'

'Another?'

'It seems everyone who could have helped our guy is dead. That's five now.'

'That seems a pretty high rate of attrition,' said Robbins. 'My suspicion radar would be going berserk if that was my case.'

'It makes you wonder, doesn't it?' said Slater. 'But two died from natural causes.'

'Are you sure about that?'

'One had terminal cancer, the other was old and had a weak heart. We've got no grounds to doubt them.'

'Well, anyway, you now know you don't need to waste your time looking for Scott Mulvaney.'

'Yes, I suppose that's true. I owe you.'

'Maybe you can buy me breakfast again sometime.'

CHAPTER THIRTY

After their long journey to Wales and back, Norman and Slater had decided to take it easy on Thursday morning and not start work until the afternoon. They were in the office now, Norman hunched over his laptop and Slater sifting through assorted paperwork related to the case.

Debbie Thomas had amassed quite a collection of newspaper cuttings relating to her brother's conviction. The crime had been committed two hundred miles away, but it wasn't every day a local woman was murdered by her husband, so the story had been big news, especially for the local newspaper. Over the following months leading up to the trial, there had been weekly updates to the story, and after the trial there had been a series of stories that had lasted several more weeks.

When Slater had begun to read through them an hour ago, he quickly realised he was learning very little new information with each additional story. He marvelled at the invention employed by the journalists and found he couldn't help but develop a grudging admiration for their ability to shamelessly rewrite the same story again, and again. The simple trick of illustrating each new version of the story with different photographs served to further disguise the fact that there was no new information.

Slater had no idea what exactly he was looking for. He was convinced Rhodri Evans was a key piece of the jigsaw, but quite how he fitted in he couldn't decide. He was hoping something in the newspaper stories might provide the clue they needed, but so far nothing had grabbed his attention.

He sighed, leaned back in his chair to stretch his back, and stared up at the ceiling, where a small spider was exploring the edge of the light fitting. He watched the spider for a minute or two until it disappeared around the far side of the light, then went back to his newspaper cuttings.

Slater had almost reached the bottom of the pile when the door opened, and Norman appeared with two mugs of tea. He tutted as he realised Slater had almost reached the last cutting.

'Are you telling me that if I'd waited five more minutes you would have made the tea?'

'I wouldn't go that far,' said Slater. 'Besides, you know you're the best tea-maker around here.'

'I guess I can't argue with that. At least if I make it myself I know it's going to be drinkable.'

He placed the two mugs on Slater's makeshift desk, carelessly spilling a few drops, making Slater tut back at him. 'I prefer it in the mug,' he said.

Norman grinned. 'Yeah, well, there's a price that has to be paid for being lazy,' he said, cheerfully. 'You want neat and tidy tea, you'll have to make it yourself. Anyway, the reason I made it is because Vinnie called.'

'About the bank account? Has he got a name? Is it someone we've interviewed?'

Norman took a folded sheet of paper from under his arm, unfolded it and placed it in front of his colleague.

Slater studied the sheet of paper. '"Joseph Linden, solicitor, Winchester",' he read. 'Is he sure about this?'

Norman looked down his nose at Slater. 'Look, I know you don't like Vinnie, but has he ever given us anything but accurate information?'

Slater was disappointed with the news, but he had to concede Norman's point. 'I didn't mean it like that. I suppose I was expecting it to be someone we already had as a suspect, not someone totally new.'

'He's just a one-man band who does small stuff, from what I can see,' said Norman. 'He has the office in Winchester, but he doesn't seem to have a website.'

'He's a bit behind the times, isn't he? I thought every business had a website these days.'

'We don't,' said Norman, pointedly.

'Well, not yet, but we will,' said Slater. 'Don't forget, we're just getting started.' He looked at the name again. 'Hang on a minute.' He started sifting through the newspaper cuttings. 'I'm sure I've just seen that name somewhere. Yeah, here it is.'

He picked a cutting from the pile and handed it to Norman. 'Look at the photo,' he told Norman. 'The smaller one that shows Steve Harris with another guy.'

Norman stared at the photograph and read out the caption. '"Murder suspect Steve Harris and his solicitor, Mr Joseph Linden". Wow! I think we can safely say there's a connection there, don't you?'

'But why the hell would he be paying Rhodri Evans to lie about Steve Harris?'

'Why don't we go and ask him?' suggested Norman.

'Let's see what we can learn about him first. He might not have a website, but that doesn't mean we can't find information about him.'

'I'll go see what I can find online.'

'I'll have another look through this stuff Debbie gave us,' said Slater.

'This guy didn't actually defend Steve in court,' Norman reminded him.

'I realise that, but if he was Steve's solicitor, he should be in this folder somewhere.'

Norman was heading for the door. 'I'll give Debbie a call and see if she can tell us anything about him.'

As Norman pulled the door closed, Slater reached for the folder Debbie Thomas had been given by the defence team.

* * *

An hour later, Norman reappeared. 'I've just been on the phone,' he said. 'Get this: according to Debbie, Joe Linden was recommended to Steve Harris by Pritchard and Harkness. But she says Linden didn't seem to do much except hand Steve's case on to the defence team. He told Steve he would be out of his depth trying to defend him, and it was his duty to stand aside and let the experts handle it.'

'That would seem to tie in with what's in this folder,' said Slater. 'He hardly gets a mention, but he would have known what was going on, right? If he was Steve's solicitor, I'm sure he would have been kept informed of any developments in his defence, wouldn't he?'

'I'm thinking he would have known enough,' agreed Norman.

'Exactly! I've been doing some digging of my own. Our new friend Joe Linden might not have his own website, but it's almost impossible to be completely invisible these days, even if you want to be. It didn't take me long to find a website that does mention him.'

'What was it? Some sort of directory?'

'He seems to avoid most of those, which is why I get the impression he doesn't want to be found.'

'That makes it difficult to earn a living, doesn't it?'

'Not if you've been made a director and shareholder in a money-spinning company.' Slater handed Norman another of the newspaper cuttings. It was a story entitled *Local Man Convicted of Wife's Murder.*

'Take a good look at the photograph. Not the wagon driving Harris away, but the figures in the background to the left.'

A man and two women could be seen in the background of the photograph.

'Aren't they a cosy little group?' said Norman.

'I'd say they were congratulating each other, wouldn't you?'

'I wonder if this is about the time he became the fourth director.'

'Yeah, I reckon that would be interesting to know, don't you? Give me half an hour and I'll see if I can find out when that happened.'

CHAPTER THIRTY-ONE

'Right,' said Slater, rubbing his hands together. 'I think we've got it.'

'You found what you were looking for?'

'I think so. It looks as if our new friend, Joe Linden, became a director of Pritchard and Harkness around the same time Rhodri Evans was buying his house.'

'What's your theory?' asked Norman.

'It looks to me as if Steve Harris has been framed. I believe he was telling the truth when he said he was at home with Eddie Smith's wife, Jackie. I also believe his car was off the road, so Rhodri Evans couldn't have seen it on that caravan site.'

'So, who killed Julie Harris? D'you think it was Rhodri?'

'I can't see it, Norm, can you? A guy like that would be too unreliable. There's too much risk he would be in a drug-fuelled stupor when he was needed.'

'In that case, you think he was being paid because he saw something?'

'That's got to be it. I think he saw the murderer at the site that weekend, and when Julie's body was found he told them what it would cost to keep him quiet.'

'So, if Linden was the go-between and we can prove the money came from Pritchard and Harkness, that narrows it down to what, four people?'

'Four people with alibis,' said Slater, 'but I'm not sure those alibis were ever tested, because the original investigation focused on Steve right from the start. No one else was ever in the frame.'

'Okay, so let's go through them,' said Norman. 'James and Sandra Harkness were both at home and vouch for each other. If they stick to their stories, that's going to be a hard one to crack.'

'Yeah, we're going to have to think about how we can test that one.'

'I guess they could have done it together.'

'Good luck with finding a motive for that,' said Slater.

'How about Amy Pritchard? At home on her own is a bit of a hard one to prove, but I can't see her murdering anyone, can you?'

'I would think she's the least likely,' agreed Slater. 'So, that just leaves John Pritchard. The others say he was up in Scotland, but what if they're covering for him? Suppose he killed Julie and they wanted to keep it quiet to protect the business.'

'I'm not so sure,' said Norman, doubtfully.

'Don't forget his suicide note. Maybe Amy was wrong, and he was actually feeling guilty about Julie's death.'

'It's not exactly cut and dried, is it? If they all stick to their stories, all we can prove is that they paid a lot of money to a guy in Wales, but they could invent any number of reasons for that, and the only guy who could tell us the truth is dead.'

'We need to find the weak link,' said Slater. 'Are we doing anything tomorrow?'

'What have you got in mind?'

'I was thinking maybe Sandra Harkness might care to answer some more questions first thing in the morning. Maybe I'll throw in a couple of bluffs as a surprise.'

CHAPTER THIRTY-TWO

Sandra Harkness was not impressed to find Slater and Norman on her doorstep before ten on a Friday morning.

'Oh, you two again. I thought I answered all your questions when you were here the other day.'

'Yes, we're sorry to bother you again, but we've got one or two more questions.'

She heaved a sigh. 'I hope this won't take long.'

Norman gave her his best understanding smile. 'I don't think it will,' he said.

'You'd better come in.'

They followed her into the lounge.

'Did you ever meet Julie Harris's husband, Steve?' asked Slater.

'I'm sorry?'

'We know for a fact he attended at least one of the company Christmas parties. Amy Pritchard was kind enough to lend us a photo album. He's there in one photo, chatting to you at the bar.'

'A lot of men used to chat with me at those parties.'

'Steve Harris had a reputation as a ladies' man, did you know that?'

'I'm not even sure I can remember him.'

'Really? Only I spoke to him on the phone earlier, and he certainly remembers you.'

She sniffed. 'He must be mistaken.'

'Is he mistaken about the mole on the inside of your right thigh, just—'

'What the hell is this?' she snapped. 'How dare you come here and make these accusations? What makes you think I would risk everything I had for such a man?'

'When we spoke to you the other day, you admitted you would have been happy to risk it all for John Pritchard if he had been just a bit more of a man,' said Slater.

'Maybe you wanted to get even with your husband,' suggested Norman.

'What on earth—'

'He was sleeping with Julie, wasn't he?' asked Slater. 'Or, at least, he wanted to. That must have got under your skin. I would think sleeping with her husband would be the perfect response for a vengeful wife.'

'Don't forget the photo we showed you before, Mrs Harkness,' said Norman. 'It looked to me like you had revenge written all over your face.'

Sandra looked daggers at Norman but again seemed at a loss for words.

'Are you really going to claim you don't know Steve Harris?' asked Norman.

She let out a long breath. 'Oh, alright. So, I saw him a couple of times. What of it?'

'Did you like him?'

'He had a certain charm, but any woman getting involved with a man like that knows what she's getting into.'

'But you liked him?'

'Yes, I liked him. There, I've said it now. Are you satisfied?'

'But if you liked him, how could you let him go to prison for something he didn't do?' asked Slater.

'What are you talking about? I had nothing to do with him going to prison. I wasn't even at the trial.'

Slater handed her a photocopy of a newspaper cutting. 'This photograph says you were there for the verdict, along with Amy Pritchard.'

She stared hard at the photograph but said nothing.

'We were wondering who that man is. The three of you seem to be congratulating each other.'

'We were probably pleased to see Julie's killer put behind bars. I'm not even sure who that man is.'

'No?' asked Norman. 'Now that does surprise me.'

She glared at him, her eyes narrowing to slits.

'I think you'd better take another look.' Slater tapped the photo. 'You see, we happen to know there are only four directors and four shareholders in your company. There's your husband, yourself, Amy Pritchard and this man is number four. We also know your company holds a board meeting on the first Friday of every month.'

'We know the board doesn't actually run the company. James makes all the decisions, isn't that right?' said Norman.

'We're also pretty confident none of you would dare miss a meeting,' added Slater. 'We think you do know that man. If you need a reminder, I can tell you that his name is Joe Linden.'

'I have no idea where you're going with this,' she said. 'But I think you should leave. Now.'

Slater ignored her and handed her a sheet of paper. She took it and stared at it.

'That's a bank statement belonging to a man named Rhodri Evans. He wasn't a very nice man, but that's neither here nor there as he's now dead. Take a look at the tenth of the month. You'll see a payment coming into his account for three thousand pounds.'

She looked up, puzzled. 'What's this got to do with me?'

'We think you're paying him every month.'

'What?' she shrieked. She looked back down at the statement. 'This money definitely isn't coming from my bank account.'

It was another bluff, but Slater was confident they had it worked out and that she would crack.

'But I don't, I mean I haven't, never . . .' She got to her feet and went across to a small writing bureau, returning with a bank statement of her own which she threw in Slater's face.

'There. That's the only bank account I have. Take the statement with you if you must. You can see my money comes in every month from Pritchard and Harkness, and you will see all my expenses. I may be a little extravagant, but I've got nothing to hide. Anyway, why would I be paying this man every month?'

'He was blackmailing you.'

'Why would he blackmail me?'

'Because you paid him a hundred grand to kill Julie Harris and then stand up in court and say he'd seen Steve Harris's car on the caravan site the day Julie died.'

Sandra had gone a strange shade of white, and her mouth hung open in shock. 'But that's just not true. I have never paid anyone anything. That's Joe Lind—'

'I'm sorry,' said Norman. 'I didn't quite catch that. Did you say, "that's Joe Linden's job"? Only that's what we figured.'

'I said no such thing. Don't try to put words into my mouth.'

'Okay, let me rephrase that . . . we think someone paid Rhodri Evans a hundred thousand pounds and thought that was the last they would see of him, but he got greedy and demanded the money kept coming every month or he would go to the police.'

Sandra started shaking her head, but then she seemed to calm down and get hold of herself. She crossed her arms and struck a defiant pose. 'I don't know what you think you're playing at, but this whole conspiracy with Joe Linden idea is absurd. And in any case, I didn't want Julie dead. I wanted her to have an affair with that bastard husband of mine, so I could divorce him!'

'But what about the payments?' said Slater.

'You're not listening to me. I already told you this money is nothing to do with me, and I know nothing about it.'

'Then who is behind it?'

'You're the detective. Why don't you tell me?'

Slater couldn't think of an answer to that. He had been confident Sandra would drop her guard and they would catch her out, but she had seen through his bluff. He looked at Norman helplessly. He was beginning to realise just how powerless they were. If they had still been police officers, they could have taken Sandra Harkness in for questioning and accessed the company bank accounts, and that was just for starters, but without those powers, there was a limit to what they could do.

Sandra smiled like someone who knew they had the upper hand. 'Now, you're not the police so you can't arrest me, and I'm quite sure you can't compel me to answer any more of your questions. Am I right?'

'Yes, I guess so,' said Norman.

'In that case, we all know where we stand, don't we?'

'What can you tell us about Joe Linden?'

'You are unbelievable, do you know that? Five minutes ago, you were sure I was guilty of bribing someone to kill Julie Harris, and now you know you've got it wrong you want me to solve your case for you? You must be joking.'

'Look, I'm sorry if we offended you, but there's an innocent man in prison, a murderer has been free for ten years, and witnesses seem to be dropping like flies. I was hoping you might be prepared to help. I guess I was wrong.'

'Have you finished?' she snapped.

Slater and Norman stood before her like two naughty schoolboys in front of their headmaster. Slater couldn't recall ever feeling so humiliated. He had been so sure she would be the weak link.

Sandra was enjoying her triumph and let them squirm for a few moments before she spoke. 'If you're looking for a murder to solve, I often wonder if poor John really committed suicide.'

'Why do you say that?' asked Slater.

'You don't know, then?'

'Know what?'

'About Amy Pritchard and my husband.'

'She's hardly his type, is she? I thought you said he's a groper? I can't imagine Amy Pritchard putting up with that sort of behaviour.'

'Good God, they don't have that sort of relationship. Mind you, if they did, I'm sure he wouldn't be like that with her. She seems to be able to control him, somehow. Maybe it's because she's older, I really don't know. But I can tell you they're as thick as thieves, believe me.'

Slater looked at Norman, but Norman's face told him he was equally confused by this revelation. 'Are you saying you think your husband could have murdered John Pritchard, and Amy knew?'

'Let me tell you, that man is a monster. He's capable of anything. And don't be fooled by Amy and her "sweet as sugar" routine. That woman is as devious as they come. I wouldn't put anything past her.'

'Have you any proof?' asked Slater.

Sandra's nostrils flared, and her face reddened. 'I don't know how you have the gall to ask that after what you've just done!'

'Look, I'm sorry. I didn't mean to—'

'Right. Good. I hope you really are sorry. Now get out! You know where the door is.'

She turned her back on them, and they quickly took the hint.

* * *

'Wow, she is one formidable lady,' said Norman, as they climbed into their car. 'Talk about fireworks. I thought she was going to explode.'

'Yeah, we certainly lit her fuse, didn't we?' said Slater. 'But as for her being the weak link, I got that totally wrong. She didn't give us anything concrete, did she? I think it would be fair to say that whole scenario didn't quite go as planned.'

'Is that what they call an understatement?' Norman put the car into gear and pulled away.

'Okay, so I made a complete balls-up.'

'Yeah, well, no one's perfect. I probably wouldn't have done any better. I thought we had it all worked out too. Anyway, we might have got the details wrong, but we're close, I'm sure of it. Joe Linden paid Rhodri Evans to do something, and it was a much bigger deal than telling a lie. If it wasn't to commit a murder, then it was to keep quiet about who did.'

Norman thought for a moment.

'I don't think Rhodri committed murder,' he said. 'He couldn't very well threaten to go to the police if he was a murderer.'

'You're right, but that must mean he knew who the murderer was.'

'So now we've found the cover-up, it pretty much narrows the field of suspects, don't you think?'

'I reckon so,' said Slater.

'What did you think about that James Harkness and Amy Pritchard thing that Sandra dropped into the conversation?'

Slater sighed. 'Pure bullshit. I could almost hear her brain whirring away as she tried to come up with some cock and bull story to throw us off the scent.'

'Yeah, that's what I thought,' said Norman. 'I'd love it to be true, but Amy and Harkness? Seriously?'

They'd been driving for a couple of minutes before Norman spoke again.

'What do you think Amy would say if we told her we thought she and James Harkness were an item?'

Slater took his eyes off the road to give Norman a quick glance. 'What?'

'Well, we just rattled Sandra's cage and got nowhere, but she knows we're on the scent, and I'm sure she's going to sound the alarm bells now, right? So why don't we see if we can get to Amy before Sandra does? And, assuming we can get there quick enough, why don't we tell her what Sandra has just suggested?'

He glanced at Slater, who was wearing a broad grin.

'You like that idea, right?' asked Norman.

Slater's grin was even wider.

'Your head will split in half if that grin gets any wider,' Norman observed.

'Yeah, whatever. Let's go and see Amy.'

CHAPTER THIRTY-THREE

Sandra's story about Amy Pritchard and James Harkness being as 'thick as thieves' was so unlikely in so many ways that Slater and Norman didn't think it could possibly be true. Nonetheless, they had decided to come right out and ask her. If they were wrong and it was true, she would be horrified they knew, and if they were right, she would be horrified they should even think such a thing. Either way, they expected a reaction, and they weren't disappointed.

'Where on earth did you hear such a thing?' she shrieked. 'I can't believe anyone would even suggest it. James Harkness, and me? The man's an animal. I avoid contact with him at all costs.'

'But you do see him once a month at the board meetings,' Norman pointed out. 'Surely you can't avoid him there.'

'One has to do one's duty.'

'I understand there are four directors,' said Slater. 'We know about James, Sandra and you, but who is the fourth?'

She studied his face for a few moments. 'I think you know very well who he is. His name is Joseph Linden. He's the company solicitor.'

'We've not met him yet,' said Slater. 'Is he a nice man?'

'If you must know, he's just like the others, and I despise all of them,' she said shortly.

'And why is that?'

'James Harkness is an animal, that scheming wife of his is nothing but a cheap tart, and that so-called solicitor is one of the slimiest characters you could meet.'

'But you tolerate them because you like the money, right?'

'I inherited those shares when my husband died. I have every right to benefit from them.'

Slater bowed his head slightly to acknowledge the truth in that fact. 'I'm curious about this board of directors,' he said. 'As I understand it, you make no business decisions, so why do you meet every month? Is there some other reason, some secret you all share, perhaps?'

Amy shook her head. 'For all his faults, James Harkness is the driving force behind the company. Apart from having the happy knack of always making the correct business decisions, he also knows how to grease the wheels. He attracts clients like pins to a magnet. I might hate him, but where this company is concerned, the directors are not foolish enough to think anyone could do a better job.'

'So, he's the golden goose,' suggested Slater.

'Yes, you could put it like that.'

'Can we go back to the weekend Julie Harris died?' asked Norman.

She rolled her eyes and let out a heavily exaggerated sigh. 'Really? Again? This was all dealt with ten years ago.'

'I'm sorry if you find this tiresome, Mrs Pritchard, but we don't believe Steve Harris killed his wife. He's had ten years of his life taken away for something he didn't do.'

'He was found guilty in a court of law,' she argued.

'He was convicted on the evidence of a man called Rhodri Evans,' said Slater.

At the mention of Rhodri Evans, Amy Pritchard's head jerked ever so slightly.

'You know the name?' asked Norman.

'I don't believe I do.'

'Oh, I think you do,' said Norman. 'You would have heard it at Steve Harris's trial.'

'I wasn't at the trial.'

Slater handed her a copy of the news story and photograph. 'Looks like you have a double. Maybe Sandra Harkness and Joe Linden have doubles too.'

They waited while she stared at the photograph.

'That is you, isn't it, Mrs Pritchard? You and two of the three people you so despise?' asked Slater. 'It looks to me like you three were pretty happy at the verdict. I wonder why that was.'

'We were probably pleased the right man got put away for killing poor Julie,' she said.

Slater looked at Norman. 'Well, there you go,' he said. 'That's exactly what Sandra Harkness said.'

'There you are, then,' said Amy. 'If Sandra says it too, it must be right. Like I said, we were happy the right man was found guilty.'

'Now that's strange,' said Norman, 'because we thought you looked happy that the wrong man was found guilty.'

'But that man saw his car on the caravan site.'

'No, Mrs Pritchard,' said Slater. 'Rhodri Evans didn't see Steve's car on the caravan site, he said he saw it. I think you'll agree that's not quite the same thing, is it?'

'But why would he say it if he didn't see it?'

'You're really going to do this, are you?' asked Slater.

'Do what?'

'Pretend you don't know what I'm talking about.'

She was desperately trying to look innocent but failing miserably.

Slater sighed. 'Alright, I'll play your little game. The reason Rhodri said he saw Steve's car was because he was paid a very large sum of money to say it. The reality is he didn't see Steve's car at all, but he did see something else.'

'I don't understand what you're talking about.'

'I think you do, but just to make it a little easier for you, I'll let you into a secret: we know Joe Linden was paying Rhodri Evans to keep quiet.'

'I know nothing about that.'

'I'm sorry, Amy, but we think you do know all about it,' said Slater. 'And we think you know exactly who killed Julie Harris. Why don't you stop playing games and tell us? We're going to find out anyway, so why don't you save us some time?'

She shook her head, slowly and wearily, but still she said nothing.

'Come on, Amy! The poor guy hasn't just served ten years, he lost a wife he loved as well. Don't you think that's enough punishment for an innocent man? What did he ever do to you?'

She bowed her head as tears began to roll down her cheeks. 'I have no idea what you're talking about. I don't know anything about any payments to anyone. Please, will you go away and leave me alone. Or shall I call the police?'

Slater looked at a very uncomfortable Norman.

'She's had enough, Dave, I think we should go,' said Norman.

Slater couldn't quite believe they had nothing to show for all his questions, but he knew they were wasting their time. He turned on his heel and marched out.

* * *

'That got pretty uncomfortable in there,' said Norman, as they drove away. 'I wish I hadn't suggested it now.'

'Don't let that sweet old lady thing fool you, Norm,' said Slater. 'They're both hiding the truth, and they're so bloody good at it because they've had so long to practice. I bet those monthly board meetings are called so they can run through their stories again and again.'

'I wish I was as sure as you are.'

'I'm right, Norm, I know I'm right. I just have to find a way of proving it.'

CHAPTER THIRTY-FOUR

It was Friday evening, and Slater's phone was ringing. He knew it was somewhere close by, but it took him a few seconds to realise it was in his jacket pocket. As he fished out the phone, a folded sheet of paper dropped out with it.

'It's Robbins. I spoke to your friend DI Williams again today. He accepted your apology.'

'I should think so, too. We helped him out, and gave him a lead,' said Slater. 'He wouldn't have had a clue where to start otherwise.'

'Would that be the caravan site owner who happens to have a cast iron alibi?'

Slater cursed quietly. 'Yeah, well, he would have, wouldn't he? I expect he paid someone else to do the dirty work.'

'Actually, DI Williams doesn't think your friend Ivor had anything to do with it. The dead man had a huge drug habit and owed an equally massive debt to his drug dealer. They found fingerprints belonging to a well-known drug dealer, and he's now in custody, answering questions, as we speak.'

'You're joking.'

'I kid you not,' said Robbins.

Slater muttered another soft curse.

'I hope you're not swearing at me.'

'What? No, of course not,' he said, hastily. 'I'm just saying goodbye to our conspiracy theory. Norm and I thought we'd worked out the solution to our case this afternoon. We thought this guy could well be another victim of our killer.'

'I'm sorry,' she said, 'I didn't mean to ruin your work.'

'Oh well, we've obviously got it wrong. At least this way we don't get to look like a pair of idiots and embarrass ourselves.'

He listened to her soft laugh for a moment. 'Sorry,' she said, again. 'I shouldn't laugh.'

'No, it's okay,' he said. 'At least when you mock me you have a pleasant laugh. I didn't expect to hear from you for a few days.'

'Yes, well, things change, don't they?'

He thought he could detect something in her voice. 'You sound a bit down,' he said. 'Has something happened?'

'No, no, I'm fine. Tell me about this case of yours.'

'It looks like our client is innocent, just as his sister claims, and he's been the victim of a cover-up.'

'But he's done ten years, hasn't he?'

'Yeah, that's right, poor sod. We're pretty sure we've got it worked out right—'

'Apart from the latest victim in Wales,' Robbins reminded him.

'Okay, we might be wrong about that bit, but we're sure there's a cover-up over the original murder. The thing is, the two women I thought would be the weak links have had ten years to practice their stories. At the moment, they know we can't touch them, but I'm determined I'm going to break one of them sooner or later.'

'I'm sure you'll get there,' she said. 'Sometimes the answer's right under your nose, you know.'

'Yeah, but if it's there this time, it's going to have to smack me in the face for me to see it.'

'Just make sure it's all legal and above board or your guy will still be stuck inside. Let me know if I can do anything to help, okay?'

'Yeah, sure. I'll bear that in mind.'

'I've got to go now. I'll call you when I've got some more news about the other matter.'

As Slater put his phone down, he remembered the piece of paper that had fallen from his pocket and reached down for it. As he slowly unfolded it, he recognised it as the bank statement Sandra Harness had thrown in his face. He was going to put it straight into the rubbish bin, but out of habit and years of training, he couldn't help but look at it first.

Five minutes later, Norman rushed into the room. 'I'm off out,' he said.

'Before you go,' said Slater, handing him the bank statement, 'take a look at this. It just smacked me in the face.'

Norman took the statement and stared at it. 'What am I looking for?'

'Fifteenth of the month, payment going out.'

Norman found the payment. 'Yes, and . . . ?'

'That's a Scottish name, right?'

'Yes.'

'D'you think you could get in touch with Vinnie?'

'Why? I thought you didn't even like him.'

'I don't like him, but I can't deny the man's a computer wizard. He could check this out in five minutes. If that's a regular payment, perhaps there's another secret up in Scotland.'

'Jeez, it's a bit of a long shot, isn't it? Are we that desperate?'

'I'm not sure about desperate, but it's going to take something pretty radical to make a breakthrough, right?'

'But we don't even know if this is relevant.'

'I don't care if it's relevant, Norm. I can't believe Sandra Harkness doesn't have any secrets. If this is one of them and it gives us a bit of leverage to use against her, I want to know what it is.'

'Well, I suppose I can ask him, but I hope you're right. I wouldn't want to piss him off by wasting his time.'

'I promise I'll make it up to him if it's a waste of time,' said Slater. 'And can you ask him to see if there are any similar, regular payments.'

'Alright, I'll call him in the morning.'

'Can't you do it now?'

'But I'm going out.'

'C'mon, Norm. It'll only take five minutes.'

Norman sighed. When Slater was in this mood he was unlikely to give up until he got his way. 'Okay, okay. I'll do it now.'

CHAPTER THIRTY-FIVE

It was eleven on Sunday morning when Slater parked his car outside the small timber lodge that served as the reception office for the Glendovie Estate in Scotland. He had driven for ten hours on Saturday, finally stopping at a small B & B just a few miles down the road from the estate to spend the night. He had completed his journey that morning after breakfast.

He looked around, but there was no sign of life, so he climbed from his car and made his way across to the office. *Please ring the bell and enter* said a sign. He pressed the bell, pushed the door open, and made his way inside. The walls were adorned with framed photographs of varied landscapes, which he assumed were taken here on the estate. While he waited, Slater amused himself by studying each in turn.

'Can I help you?' asked a voice.

Slater turned to find a rugged-looking man, he guessed to be in his sixties, had entered through a door on the other side of the room. He was looking at Slater with suspicion.

'Good morning,' said Slater.

'I don't think I recognise your face,' said the man.

'No, I've not been here before.'

'I need to know who you're with, only I've not been notified to expect any newcomers. I can't allow you on the estate if you're not authorised.'

'Is it only companies that own the lodges?' asked Slater.

'There are a few individuals, but it's mostly companies who lease them.'

'Ah, so they're leased, not owned. Is one leased to a company called Pritchard and Harkness?'

Now the man folded his arms. 'You ask a lot of questions, don't you?'

'It's my job to ask questions,' said Slater.

'And it's my job to protect the privacy of the people who stay here. Who are you, the police?'

'My name's Dave Slater. I'm a private investigator. I'm looking for a man called Robbie McGregor who works here on the estate. Is that you?'

The man seemed to relax a little, and the ghost of a smile crossed his face. 'A private investigator? In that case, I don't have to answer any of your questions, do I?'

'No, you don't have to, but I think you might want to.'

The man smiled more obviously now and shook his head. 'I don't think so.'

'You are McGregor, aren't you?' said Slater. 'You look after the lodges here. I bet you see some things, don't you? I bet you know a few secrets, eh?'

'I think you might want to bugger off back to England before I call the police.'

'Now why would you think that?'

'Because this is private property and you're not wanted around here.'

Slater unfolded a sheet of paper from his pocket and held it out to the man. 'You might want to take a look at this before you make that call.'

'What's that?'

'Here, take it. I think you'll find it quite interesting.'

McGregor reached for the sheet of paper and looked at it. Then he looked up at Slater. 'This is my bank statement. How the hell did you get hold of this?'

Slater smiled. 'Do you still want to call the police?'

'And why wouldn't I?'

'Payment coming in on the fifteenth of the month. It comes from Sandra Harkness, and it comes every month.'

McGregor looked down at the statement again. The tips of his ears were pink.

'Pritchard and Harkness lease a lodge here on the estate, don't they?' asked Slater.

'Mr Harkness leases a lodge here.'

'It's a private lodge, not a company one?'

'Aye.'

'And Mrs Harkness comes here on her own?'

'Sometimes, aye.'

'Why is she paying you?'

'I look out for her, keep an eye on their lodge.'

'But isn't that what you do anyway? Isn't that your job?'

'Aye, but I go that little bit extra for her lodge.'

'Nice try, McGregor, but there are four more like that. Are you telling me you do that little bit extra for all of them? Or are they paying for your silence? I reckon that's more likely, don't you?'

McGregor was looking distinctly nervous. 'Look,' he said, 'it's just a few pounds extra to make ends meet. I deserve more than the pittance I get paid for doing this job.'

'D'you still want to call the police?' asked Slater. 'Only I'd be happy to let them know they should check you out. They might even be interested in what some of these people have been up to.'

'Christ, don't do that, I'd lose my job!' said McGregor, desperately.

'Don't panic. I haven't come up here to make you lose your job. Quite frankly, I don't give a damn about your little enterprise. I'm only interested in one of your victims.'

'Which one?'

'I want to know what you have on Sandra Harkness. You tell me what she's got to hide, and I'll clear off. You'll never see me again.'

Slater could almost hear McGregor's brain working as he considered his options. 'I can promise you she's not going to be paying you for much longer anyway, so you might as well tell me.'

'I don't have much choice, do I?'

Slater smiled. 'No choice at all. You know it makes sense.'

CHAPTER THIRTY-SIX

'Stella Robbins,' said the voice in Slater's ear.

'It's Dave Slater.'

'If you're hoping for more news, I haven't got any yet.'

'That's not why I'm calling.'

'You sound weird. Where are you?'

'I'm sitting in my car outside a bed and breakfast somewhere just south of the border between England and Scotland.'

'Scotland! Whatever are you doing all the way up there?'

'It's a long story, but the short version is I needed to speak to a man.'

'Is there something wrong with using a telephone?'

'If I had done that, he could easily have refused to speak to me and hung up. There was only one way I could guarantee he wouldn't do that.'

'I would have needed one hell of a good reason to make a journey like that.'

Slater thought it might be best to avoid telling her about Norman's friend, Vinnie, and how he had hacked into someone's bank account.

'It was a hunch.'

'My God, that's one powerful hunch if it makes you drive from one end of the UK to the other and back.'

'Yeah, well, that's my impulsive nature, I guess. Anyway, I had nothing else to do this weekend.'

'Oh, right. You make a habit of driving for days at a time when you've got nothing to do, do you? Driving non-stop for hours is a good way of killing yourself.'

'Which is precisely why I'm outside a bed and breakfast. I've got nothing to rush back for so I'm about to book in for the night. I'll make my way back tomorrow when I wake up. It's one of the joys of not being an employee.'

'Is that why you called? Just to tell me how lucky you are working for yourself?'

'I hadn't thought of that,' he said, 'but, no, that's not it. The real reason is that you said the other day to let you know if you could help in any way.'

'You mean help with your case?'

'Yeah. Were you for real?'

'What have you got in mind?'

'How about arresting a murderer? I suppose me and Norm could make a citizen's arrest, but it would be much better if—'

'I can't go around arresting people for murder just because you say so.'

'I know that. But what if we got a confession for you?'

'And how are you going to do that?'

'One of us could wear a wire.'

'I think you've been watching too many TV shows. You were in the police. You know it's never that easy to get permission to do these things.'

'Oh, come on, Stella. I'm offering you a murderer on a plate. Are you going to turn that down?'

'I don't know.'

'Okay, suit yourself,' said Slater. 'We can do it the hard way. It's no problem. I just thought, after having the other case taken away from you . . .'

'I'll have to talk to my boss, but I can promise you he won't be easy to convince.'

'Think about it,' said Slater. 'I have to go now. Bye.'

'Hang on—'

Slater ended the call before she could say any more. If he was right, she would be chomping at the bit to catch a murderer, and he was confident she would call him back at some stage tomorrow.

CHAPTER THIRTY-SEVEN

Despite spending Saturday and Sunday nights in hotel rooms, Slater had found it necessary to make frequent coffee stops on the journey back, and he had been utterly shattered by the time he had arrived home on Monday evening.

Such was his weariness, he had spent nearly all of Tuesday sleeping, but at least he knew it had been worth it. Now it was Wednesday morning, and he was fully recovered and wide awake. He, and Norman, were on their way to Pritchard and Harkness. It was time to speak to James Harkness again.

* * *

It was clear the receptionist recognised the two detectives as they marched into the building, and she didn't look pleased to see them.

'We'd like to speak with James Harkness, please,' said Norman.

'I'm afraid that won't be possible.'

'Is he out?' asked Slater.

'No, he's in a meeting.'

'I'm sure he won't mind making time for us,' said Norman.

'He can't be disturbed.'

'Why not?'

'Because it's a board meeting.'

Norman nudged Slater with his elbow. 'Oh, really? So that means all four directors are there, right?'

'Yes, of course. But the directors cannot be disturbed during a meeting. It's a company rule.'

'That's okay, don't you worry,' Norman assured her. 'We won't disturb anyone. We'll go on up and wait outside.'

Before she could protest any further, they rushed off up the stairs. They knew from when they had been here before that the boardroom was on the first floor, next door to James Harkness's office.

'Can you believe that?' said Norman, as they hurried up the stairs. 'All four of them up there together.'

'It's an unexpected bonus. I thought we'd have to round them all up one at a time. Now, this should be really interesting. I can't wait to see what happens when we start making accusations.'

'I thought this was going to be fun before, but now there's going to be four of them. I can't wait to see their faces when we walk in!'

They didn't break step at the top of the stairs, striding across to the boardroom and barging in without warning. They could hear James Harkness speaking as they entered the room, but he stopped in mid-sentence as they appeared.

'You two!' he spluttered. 'What the hell do you think you're doing barging in here like this?'

Harkness was at the head of the massive table, with Joe Linden nearby. The two women had kept their distance from the two men and were sitting, open-mouthed, with the table between each other.

'My, my, doesn't this look cosy?' said Slater. 'What is it? Boys against girls? But then even you two girls don't seem to be on the same side, do you?'

'This is extravagant, isn't it?' asked Norman. 'You have four directors on the board and a table that would easily seat twelve. Or is it this big so you can keep your distance from each other?'

'What do you want?' asked Harkness. 'Can't you see we're in a meeting?'

'Oh, yeah, we can see,' said Slater. 'But this isn't your normal monthly meeting, so I'm wondering why you're all here today? Has someone been asking too many questions and getting too close to the truth for comfort?'

'I have no idea what you're talking about,' said Harkness.

'No, of course, you haven't.'

'Our guess is that this little get-together is just to make sure you're all still singing from the same hymn sheet,' said Norman.

Sandra Harkness had been wide-eyed with shock when they had walked in, but now she had regained some of her composure. 'This is outrageous,' she snapped. 'We've been prepared to help with your enquiries up until now, but this time you've gone too far. I think you should leave.'

'Ah, yes, Mrs Harkness,' said Norman. 'I've got to be honest and admit you have been very helpful, but there was something you said last time we spoke that's been nagging away at us.'

'A couple of things, actually,' added Slater.

'That's right, a couple of things. You know what we're talking about, don't you?'

She kept her face deadpan. 'I have no idea.'

'We'll remind you in a minute,' said Norman. He turned to face Amy Pritchard. 'And then we have the lovely Mrs Pritchard. I have to admit, you had me fooled the other day. I almost felt sorry for you, especially when those tears appeared, but, of course, everyone knows crocodile tears mean nothing.'

'Crocodile tears? What on earth are you talking about?' she cried.

'And then there's this story you told us about how John committed suicide because he felt guilty about the way he had treated you.'

'Why else would he kill himself?'

'How about because he killed Julie Harris?' Slater said.

The two women looked horrified.

'Preposterous!' said Harkness. 'John was in Scotland.'

'Oh, yeah, that's right,' said Norman. 'John was in Scotland, on his own. That's the story you four concocted and then told everyone, isn't it?'

'It's not a story, it's true,' said Amy.

'And you believe that, do you?' asked Slater.

'Why shouldn't I believe it? It's the truth. Why on earth would you have reason to doubt it?'

'I'm just going to get to that,' said Slater. 'But first, why don't we let Mr Linden explain why he paid a guy called Rhodri Evans a hundred grand to say he'd seen Steve Harris's car at the caravan site the night Julie Harris died?'

'Rubbish!' said Linden.

'We've got a copy of your bank statement that says it isn't,' said Norman.

'How on earth did you get that?'

Harkness looked aghast. 'You used your own bank account?' he blurted out. 'You bloody idiot!'

'I did as you asked,' said Linden.

'I didn't tell you to use your own bloody bank account!'

Norman beamed a big smile at the two men. 'Oh, wow, I didn't expect a team that's been practising for ten years to start falling apart quite so quickly.'

Amy Pritchard was weeping quietly.

'Come on, Amy. There's a poor guy in prison who hasn't just served ten years, he lost a wife he loved as well. Don't you think that's enough punishment for an innocent man? What did he ever do to you four?'

'Yeah, that's what I don't understand,' said Slater. 'Why pick on the poor guy?'

Amy bowed her head as tears slowly rolled down her cheeks.

'That was Sandra's idea,' she said, finally. 'I felt I had no choice but to agree, you see.'

Slater and Norman exchanged a glance. They would let Amy talk in her own time. There was no need to say anything.

'John had always been such a sad man. He suffered from depression. I suppose I should have seen it coming, but I thought he had everything under control. The birdwatching seemed to help him relax, and work was going well. I knew he had a soft spot for Julie, but I had no idea it had gone beyond that.'

Slater looked at Norman and raised his eyebrows. Norman shrugged. This wasn't quite what they were expecting to hear, but it made interesting listening.

'When they told me what John had done, I couldn't believe it. And the business was doing so well. We had to keep that going, so we decided I shouldn't rock the boat, and I mustn't challenge John about it. I agreed because I was frightened it would push him over the edge, or that he might even turn on me.'

Norman couldn't let this go any further without speaking. 'Are you saying your husband, John Pritchard, killed Julie Harris?'

She looked up at him, her eyes wide. 'Yes, of course. That's why he killed himself. He couldn't live with the guilt any longer, but he couldn't confess or the whole business could have come tumbling down.'

'Shut up, you silly cow,' snapped Sandra. 'They don't know anything.'

'Don't you talk to me like that, you stupid little tart! It's alright for you two. I've had enough of all these lies.'

'Think of the business,' said Harkness. 'That's what this is really about.'

'Oh, damn your bloody business!' said Amy. 'It's not about the business. It's about that poor man who's been in prison for ten years. I can't live with it any longer.'

'Go ahead, Mrs Pritchard,' said Norman. 'What is it you want to tell us?'

'Steve Harris didn't kill Julie. It was my husband, John. We told everyone he had been birdwatching at the lodge in Scotland, but he wasn't. The cover-up is all my fault. I begged the others to help.'

'We thought John was in Scotland that weekend,' said Slater.

Amy shook her head. 'We agreed to say he was in Scotland, but he wasn't really.'

'So, you're saying John wasn't in Scotland at all, and the rumours about him and Julie going to the caravan that weekend are true, is that right?' asked Norman.

She nodded sadly. 'Yes, that's right.'

'Where did these rumours come from?' asked Slater.

'Apparently they were going around the office. James told me about them.'

'But you didn't hear them yourself?'

'I didn't work here. How could I have heard them?'

'I think even if you had been working here, you wouldn't have heard them, Mrs Pritchard,' said Slater. 'You wouldn't have heard them because those rumours never existed.'

'What? I don't understand,' she stammered. 'In his suicide note he said he couldn't cope with the guilt any more. I told you I thought he felt guilty about the way he treated me, but really he was guilty about Julie.'

Sandra Harkness had gone very quiet and was studying the table.

'What do you think, Sandra?' asked Slater.

'What?' she asked, looking up at him.

'What do you think John was feeling guilty about?'

'John was a decent man. I can't imagine he killed Julie on purpose, but I'm sure his guilt would have got the better of him.'

'You think so?' asked Slater. 'I wonder what Robbie McGregor would think.'

Sandra's face had been pale already, but now she turned an almost translucent white. Then, as Slater and Norman stared at her, she began to turn redder and redder. She tried to speak, but no words came out, and Slater was reminded of a fish out of water gulping for air.

'Who on earth is Robbie McGregor?' asked Amy.

She looked at Harkness and Linden. Linden seemed equally confused, but Harkness wouldn't look at her.

'Sandra knows Robbie, don't you, Sandra?' said Slater. 'She pays him two hundred quid every month to keep his mouth shut.'

Slater watched James Harkness slump back in his chair and raise his eyes skywards. Amy was looking increasingly puzzled.

'You've always claimed John was in Scotland, haven't you, Amy?' asked Slater.

'That's what we agreed,' she said. 'If anyone asked, we would say he was in Scotland.'

'But you didn't know for sure if he was or he wasn't?'

'He can't have been in Scotland if he was with Julie in Wales, can he?'

'Why don't we ask Sandra?' Slater said.

'What do you mean? Sandra knows the same as me.'

Norman looked sympathetically at Amy. 'You really don't know, do you, Amy?'

'Know what?'

'Are you going to tell her Sandra? Or shall I?'

Sandra looked daggers at Norman but said nothing.

Norman sighed. 'Okay. I'll do it.' He looked at Amy as if trying to decide how best to break the news. 'Amy, you've always thought John was a good man, who made a big mistake with Julie and died of a guilty conscience, am I right?'

She nodded, still confused.

'Then you're probably going to find this hard to believe,' continued Norman. 'You see, I don't think he wrote his suicide note because he was feeling guilty about you, nor was he feeling guilty about killing Julie. He was feeling guilty about the way he had betrayed you, and because he knew who Julie's killer was.'

'But John killed Julie, didn't he?' asked Amy.

'I've had enough of this!' roared Harkness. 'I want you two out of here now, or—'

'Or what?' asked Slater, lifting his eyebrows.

'I'll call the police. I'll have you thrown out.'

'I don't think so, do you?' Slater wasn't what anyone would call big and hard, but he was much fitter and stronger than Harkness. The older man backed down.

'Sit there and shut up,' said Slater. 'You'll get your chance to speak later.'

He nodded to Norman to continue.

'Now, where was I? Oh yes, I was going to explain.'

'Explain what?' asked Amy, who was struggling to keep up with what was going on.

'Why did you accept John was in Wales with Julie?' Norman asked her.

'I told you — because James and Sandra told me.'

'Right, but didn't you ever ask John?'

'He would never speak about it. Not that we ever spoke much about anything after that.'

'Why wouldn't he speak about it?'

'Because I had agreed with James and Sandra that it might push him over the edge. Mind you, I made it clear I didn't like the idea of harbouring a murderer, and that I was only doing it to save the business.'

'So, in effect, you threw your lot in with James and Sandra against your own husband? The man you say you loved.'

'I protected my husband. We all protected him by agreeing to say he was in Scotland. I've had to live with that lie for ten years.'

'But it wasn't a lie,' said Norman, gently. 'He was in Scotland. Ask Sandra. She knows he was there.'

'How could she . . . How do you know this is true?'

'I went up to Scotland and had a little chat with a man called Robbie McGregor,' explained Slater. 'He looks after the lodges. He knew nothing about the murder, but he did know John had been with Sandra that weekend. Sandra has been paying him every month since then to keep quiet about it.'

'She knows now, Sandra,' said Slater. 'So why don't you tell Amy what really happened that weekend.'

Sandra looked from Slater to Norman, then bowed her head as she spoke. 'We'd never done it before,' she began. 'We'd thought about going away for a weekend together a couple of times, but Amy used to watch him like a hawk, so it was difficult. But my husband' — she spat those two words out through gritted teeth — 'was behaving like a complete bastard at that time. I just wanted to spend a couple of days with someone who would be nice to me and treat me like a lady.'

'Scotland's a long way to go for a weekend,' said Slater.

'I went for a week, Wednesday to Wednesday. We thought it would be more convincing if I went for a week. John came up to join me for a long weekend.'

'He wasn't birdwatching?'

'He brought all his gear, but it was just for show.'

'And this was the weekend Julie Harris died?'

'Yes, it was.'

Amy's mouth had dropped open, and she stared hard at Sandra, as if unable to make sense of what she was hearing.

Sandra was quiet for a moment, then spoke again. 'I've always regretted that weekend, we both did.'

'But why?' asked Norman.

'Poor John was so sure he wanted to cheat on Amy, and then when it came to it, he couldn't.' She turned to Amy. 'He really did love you, you know. I told him it didn't matter, and he should forget about me and go back home, but he was devastated. He could never look me in the face again after that. I felt terrible for him.'

In Amy's head, the dots had apparently just all connected. 'But if John was with you, he couldn't have been in Wales.'

Sandra said nothing but gave the tiniest shrug.

'James?' said Amy. 'You told me it was John who had killed Julie. I trusted you. What have you done to me? And what about poor John?'

'Poor John, my arse,' said Harkness, thumping the table. 'He was a bloody waste of space. He was holding this company back, and don't tell me it's not true. Look at how much money we've made since he's been gone!'

‘Wait a minute,’ said Amy. ‘If that little tart was in Scotland with John, she couldn’t have been at home with you. You were the one in Wales with Julie!’

Harkness ignored her accusing stare.

‘Yeah, well worked out, Amy,’ said Slater. ‘And that’s why the creepy Mr Linden here paid Rhodri Evans a hundred thousand pounds. You see, Rhodri lived on site, and we think he had seen James with Julie that weekend. When the murder was discovered, he quickly put two and two together and realised he knew who had murdered her. That’s when he came up with the idea of asking James to pay him to keep his mouth shut.’

‘That’s rubbish,’ said Harkness. ‘You can’t prove anything, and I know nothing about any payments made by Linden.’

‘Oh, yes, you bloody well do,’ snapped Linden. ‘You’re the one going down for murder, not me. Don’t think you’re going to leave me in the bloody lurch.’

‘John needn’t have killed himself,’ said Amy. ‘I would have forgiven him for almost cheating on me. He had no reason to feel guilty.’

‘I hate to disappoint you, Amy, but I can think of a couple more reasons,’ said Norman. ‘He must have known about the bribe that was paid to Rhodri Evans to lie about Steve Harris, and he probably knew who really killed Julie Harris. That’s a terrible amount of guilt for a decent man to have to carry around.’

‘We’re pretty sure John would have known James had killed Julie,’ said Slater, ‘but maybe Sandra and James had told him they would blame him if he spoke up.’

‘That’s terrible. Poor John. I knew he couldn’t have killed Julie.’

‘Just a minute, Amy. Before you fill your sails with righteous indignation, I think you should remember you were convinced enough to have been part of this conspiracy for the last ten years.’

‘But I’ve done nothing wro—’

‘You believed John had killed Julie.’

'But you just said he didn't!' she cried.

'Don't you try to play the innocent victim, you old witch,' snarled Sandra. 'You were as happy to frame Steve Harris as the rest of us, as long as it meant keeping the money rolling in!'

'Why did you choose Steve Harris?' asked Slater.

'That was Sandra's idea,' said Amy.

Slater looked at Sandra. He was sure he could read her face. 'Let me guess. He wasn't interested in you, was he? You chose him because he rejected you.'

'We chose him,' interrupted James Harkness, 'because it was common knowledge he mistreated Julie.'

'You see?' said Amy. 'These two planned the whole thing. I was never a willing party to this conspiracy. I had no choice.'

'There's always a choice, Amy,' said Slater. 'You chose to accept John was guilty, and you were happy to keep it a secret. You knew Steve Harris had been framed, and I'm sure you must have known about the first payment to Rhodri Evans. I can't believe you didn't know about the monthly payments after he got greedy, either.'

'I didn't know he was being paid to keep quiet about James!'

'No, you thought he had been paid because he had seen John, but it makes no difference. You still knew he was being paid to lie in court and convict an innocent man.'

'I know nothing about that.'

'Yeah, right. You can put it in your statement to the police.' Slater pulled a police radio from his pocket.

'Police? You're not the police,' snapped Harkness.

'You're right, we're not the police, but we know a detective inspector who's more than happy to step in and take over from us. She's outside now, waiting for me to call her.'

He pressed the button and put the radio to his ear. 'Did you get all that?' he said into the radio. 'Yeah. Good. Oh, they're all here, very eager to talk to you.'

* * *

'I suppose we're going to have to tell Debbie we've proved her brother is innocent,' said Slater, later. 'It's funny she hasn't been chasing us for information.'

'Actually, I thought you might prefer it if I handled that, so I've been keeping her up to date,' said Norman.

'Oh, really?'

'Is that a problem?' asked Norman.

Slater thought about it. Then he gave Norman a sad little smile.

'No, Norm, it's not a problem. To be honest, I'm not sure I want to see her.'

'I can understand that. I'm sure I'd be the same. I'm happy to go tell her what's happened.'

'Are you sure?'

'We're partners, right? That means we share the load. I've got this, okay?'

CHAPTER THIRTY-EIGHT

It was just before five on Thursday afternoon. Slater was sitting at home, wondering what he was going to do now the case was closed, when his phone started to ring.

'It's Robbins,' said the now familiar voice. 'I thought you'd like an update on our progress.'

'Have they all confessed?'

'That pompous oaf Harkness is claiming Sandra and Linden are framing him, but they're both adamant he confessed to murdering Julie Harris, and that's why they paid Rhodri Evans to keep quiet.'

'But why did he kill her?'

'Honestly? I think Julie got down there and had second thoughts,' said Robbins. 'That would be enough for a man with an ego the size of his.'

'D'you think you can make it stick?' asked Slater.

'I think so. There's too much evidence for him to get away with it, and the others will be charged with conspiracy at the very least. We're actually going to work with your friend DI Williams down in Wales, as it was their case originally.'

'I suppose that seems only fair,' said Slater.

'There seems to be some evidence missing, though.'

'Oh yeah, what's that?'

'Bank statements from Rhodri Evans, Sandra Harkness and Joe Linden.'

Slater felt a twinge of guilt, but only a tiny twinge.

'That's funny,' he said. 'They were all together. I'm sure we gave them to you.'

'Funny how they should all have gone missing, don't you think?'

'Yeah, it's pretty weird. I'll have a look around the office, see if I can find them.'

There was a brief silence, but Slater knew she was fishing, and he resisted the temptation to say any more.

'Don't worry, it's not a big deal,' said Robbins. 'We'll be going through all of their accounts anyway. It was lucky they happened to be lying around so conveniently for you, just when you needed them.'

'I guess we were lucky.'

'Yes,' she said, doubtfully. 'You were, weren't you?'

Slater kept his mouth firmly closed.

'Anyway,' she continued, when it was clear he wasn't going to fill in any of the blanks for her, 'that's the good news.'

'That sounds ominous,' said Slater. 'What's the bad news.'

'This afternoon I had to attend a meeting.'

'What does that mean?'

'I was asked to explain my actions over the last week or so regarding certain CCTV and ANPR searches.'

'Oh, crap!' said Slater. 'Does that mean what I think it means?'

'If you mean, is there a big boot headed towards my arse, I think that's probably a fair assessment.'

'Bloody hell, Stella, I didn't mean for this to happen.'

He realised he'd just used her first name, but if she objected, she didn't say.

'Oh, don't blame yourself. I knew what I was getting into.'

'How bad will it be?'

'We're reconvening tomorrow afternoon.'

'Have you been suspended from duty?'

Robbins sighed. 'They call it gardening leave,' she said. 'It's not quite as bad, but it doesn't sound promising, does it?'

'Seriously, though, what's the outcome likely to be?'

'The worst-case scenario is I get my marching orders.'

Slater felt empty inside. 'Christ, what will you do if that happens?'

'Well, first, I'll cry my eyes out, then I'll take my mum's dog for a walk.'

'I don't know how you can joke about it.'

'Who's joking?' she said. 'Didn't you tell me there's always a silver lining? Well, that's the one I'm clinging to at the moment. Me, the dog and somewhere peaceful to walk. It usually works.'

Slater was struggling to think of something he could say that would make things better, but, of course, he couldn't.

'I know it sounds pretty trite, but I'm sorry, Stella. I never wanted anything like this to happen.'

'Maybe it won't be so bad,' she said, with false bravado. 'Perhaps they'll slap my wrist and tell me not to be naughty again.'

Slater could only hope she was right. 'Look, you will give me a call and let me know what happens, won't you?' he asked.

'You're not going to offer me a job, are you?'

'Ha! I wish. There's barely enough work here for one now we've handed this case over to you lot. You will call me, though, right?'

'D'you really want to know?'

'Yes, I do. I feel responsible.'

'Please don't. I always make my own decisions, and I made this one. Any blame should be attached to my foolish pride, not to you.'

'Maybe,' he said, 'but is it foolish to have principles? I've done the same sort of thing myself in the past.'

'Yes, so I've heard. No offence, but that's not exactly a comforting thought.'

'I was just saying there's nothing wrong with having principles. I have them.'

'Yes, exactly,' she said. 'And look where it's got you.'

'Ooh, that's a bit below the belt.'

'You're right, it is. I'm sorry, I guess I'm not at my best right now.'

'That's okay, I get it,' said Slater.

'I'll let you know when I know,' she said.

The line went dead, and Slater felt another rush of guilt, but then he thought about it and realised he hadn't asked her to do this for him. As she had said, it had been her idea.

Even so, he still felt terrible about it.

CHAPTER THIRTY-NINE

Someone was hammering on Slater's front door, and he wondered who it could be at nine a.m. on a Saturday. He swung the door open to find Watson standing on his front step.

'Sam! You won't believe how pleased I am to see you,' he said. 'Thank God you're alright.'

He took a step towards her and was about to place his hands on her shoulders to kiss her cheek when he realised her face was telling him maybe she wasn't equally pleased to see him. He hastily withdrew his hands and took a step back.

'Sam? What's the matter?'

'What's the matter? What do you think is the matter?'

'Come in,' he said. 'You're obviously upset about something.'

He stepped back to let her in, and as she passed him, she spoke again. 'Yes, I am upset about something,' she said. 'And that something is you!'

'What have I done?'

'I told you to leave me alone, to stay out of it.'

'Yeah, but—'

'Not only do you keep on calling me, you even had the nerve to go and harass my sister!'

'I didn't harass anyone,' said Slater, indignantly. 'You wouldn't answer my calls, and I was worried about you. What else was I supposed to do?'

'You could have done as I asked and minded your own business. Who do you think you are?'

'I'm the bloke who spent two weeks in Thailand with you, and then lent you my car to get home, that's who I am.'

'That doesn't mean you own me.'

'I don't think I own you, and if anyone has a right to be indignant it's me, not you!'

'You should have kept out of it. Why do you think I didn't answer your calls?'

'Keep out of it? How the hell could I do that? You seem to forget you used a car exactly like mine as a decoy. I had two police officers turn up showing me photographs of what appeared to be my car blown to bits! Did you think I wouldn't want to know what the hell was going on?'

'You don't know how much trouble you've caused me,' she snapped.

'The trouble I've caused you?' said Slater, incredulously. 'Give me a break. I'm the one who got dragged into a murder investigation. I was a possible suspect, for Christ's sake. And, apart from all that, as far as I knew you still had my car, so it seemed quite reasonable to assume you may have been hurt. I was worried about you.'

'But I wasn't hurt!'

'How was I supposed to know that?'

'I told you over the phone. Wasn't that good enough?'

'It might have been if you'd explained, but you told me almost nothing.'

'I couldn't tell you anything. My boss is going potty because of you and that DI Robbins. I suppose it was your idea to get her to poke her nose in after the case was closed, was it?'

'Maybe if you hadn't used a car just like mine, with my registration plates . . .'

'Oh, don't worry, I realise what a mistake that was!'

'So, why did you?'

'Because that man followed me all the way back to London from Gatwick.'

'You mean the Russian guy, Lenkov?'

She nodded. 'We believe he's the guy who planted the bomb that killed my sister. We made sure he knew I was looking for him in the hope he would try to do the same to me. As he knew which car I was driving, we thought the best way to draw him out into the open would be if I used the same car again, and sure enough, we were right, he followed me.'

'But why didn't you tell me all this before? If I'd known, I wouldn't have needed to keep calling. I might even have been able to steer Robbins away.'

'I couldn't tell you. It just wasn't possible.'

'You said "we". So, you weren't acting alone, then?'

'Of course not.'

'But if you wanted to bump him off, why not do it quietly in London? Why bring him all the way down here to my patch?'

'You don't own Winchester. It's not your patch.'

'You know what I mean. This is my area, and anyway, it was inevitable the police would track the number plates back to me. You should have known that.'

'It wasn't supposed to play out the way it did. The police shouldn't even have known about it.'

'It doesn't matter how you dress it up, Sam. You used a mock-up of my car to murder a guy, and then you kept me in the dark. You can hardly blame me for being pissed off.'

She shook her head. 'We didn't commit murder!'

'I saw the photographs of the body. Are you trying to tell me that was some elaborate hoax that managed to fool a detective inspector and a pathologist?'

'He wasn't supposed to die.'

Slater studied her face. He wasn't convinced. 'According to Robbins, the bomb was detonated by another device that was already under the car.'

'Do you seriously think a guy who plants bombs for a living would fall for that? The second device was his. We didn't know it, but he always plants a smaller device as a failsafe in case the main one doesn't detonate.

'We watched, and waited, while he planted the bomb. We even filmed him doing it, then we moved in to arrest him. The idea was to grab him, remove the bomb, drive the car back to London, and no one would have known a thing. It should have been a simple, straightforward arrest, but that's where it all went pear-shaped. We didn't realise he would rather blow himself up.'

Slater still wasn't sure what to believe. 'He pressed the button when he saw you coming?'

She nodded. 'It made it a bit difficult to drive the car back and pretend nothing had happened.'

'So, you decided to run off and leave me to carry the can,' said Slater.

'It wasn't like that. There was no time to do anything. We just had to get out before the police arrived.'

'Yeah, like I said, leaving me to carry the can.'

'Look, I'm sorry. You have to believe me when I say there was nothing I could tell you. It's my job. The police should have been more thorough. If they had been, they would have known it wasn't your car.'

'If you hadn't left the number plates, they would have had to be more thorough,' said Slater, 'but in the circumstances, I don't blame them at all. They did the right thing.'

She said nothing, so Slater continued. 'You should have told me.'

'I have to follow orders. I couldn't tell anyone.'

'So, you do work for MI5?'

'I can hardly deny it now, can I?'

'Was Norm right about you being undercover when we first met?'

She nodded. 'Yes, I'm sorry.'

'Has it all been a sham, then?'

'Sorry?'

'You and me? Did I mean something to you? Or was I just a part of your alter-ego's background story?'

She smiled a sad smile.

'When Bradshaw first appointed you, I didn't know if I could trust you, and even if I had known, I couldn't have said anything.'

Slater wasn't quite sure if he should be angry, or sad, or what!

'I have to admit you were bloody good,' he said. 'I had no idea you were playing me all that time.'

'It wasn't like that, at all. I liked you straight away. Believe me there were some nights in those hotel rooms when I would happily have come to your room.'

'You never said.'

'Nor did you.'

'I was trying to be professional,' said Slater.

'So was I. And I couldn't afford to take the risk. I couldn't be certain about you, and if I had dropped my guard . . .'

'So, what changed?'

'When Bradshaw was brought down, I knew for sure you were one of the good guys.'

'So, Thailand?'

'Was one of the best times I've ever had,' she said. 'I just wish I could have told you everything.'

Slater thought about Thailand, and her sister, and the cute little girl he had met.

'Well, I know it all now, don't I? We could always start again.'

She shook her head, slowly. 'I don't think so.'

'If it's the job, you could quit.'

'I'm sorry,' she said. 'I like you a lot, but I love my job. I would probably end up resenting you, and I wouldn't want that.'

'You're saying that's it, then? We're finished?'

'I'm sorry.'

She walked over to stand inches from him, reached forward, and gently kissed him on the lips. Then she turned and walked across to his front door where she turned to offer another sad smile.

'Try to remember the good times, and don't be angry with me,' she said.

He watched, sadly, as she slipped through the door and pulled it closed behind her.

* * *

It had been twenty minutes since Watson had left. As he sipped at a cup of tea, Slater stared blankly out of the window. He felt empty. He could think of about a dozen things he could, and probably should, have said but, of course, these things never come to mind at the right time, do they?

These last few days had been a serious test for his new adult self and, all things considered, he supposed he had handled the situation pretty well. He thought it was even possible that, in a couple of days or so, he might be able to convince himself there were positives to be taken from it all. Right now, though, it didn't feel that way.

As he stared absently through the window at nothing in particular, he found he was thinking about how it was he could never get it right when it came to women. Watson had certainly been different, and for a while there he had even thought they might have a future together but, here he was, on his own again.

He concluded perhaps Norman was right, and he had a problem making a commitment. Even if it wasn't him, this latest entanglement had left him feeling bruised and battered enough to decide he needed a rest. He resolved he would avoid all women until further notice. Maybe he would even become a confirmed bachelor. At least then he couldn't get it wrong again, could he?

His thoughts were interrupted by another knock on the front door, although this time it was a far gentler sound. He approached the door somewhat gingerly and hesitated before he opened it, wondering who it might be. He held his breath and swung the door open.

The woman standing before him was wearing jeans, wellies, a waxed jacket, and an over-sized bobble hat. He had never seen this particular woman dressed in this way, so it was a second or two before he recognised her. Then she smiled and that confirmed it.

'Stella! What are you doing here?'

'You look as if you were expecting someone else.'

'Not really. I had a visitor earlier, but I don't think I'll be seeing her again.'

'Would that be your girlfriend, by any chance?'

'If you mean Watson, I think we can safely say it's official she's definitely not my girlfriend.'

'Oh, I'm sorry. You've had a rough morning, then?'

'Yeah, you could say that.'

'That woman has a lot to answer for. She's the one who kicked up a stink about me at work.'

'Actually, I don't think that was her. It was someone higher up the food chain.'

'You're defending her, now?'

'Let's say, having spoken to her this morning, I have a much better understanding of her situation. It was very difficult for her.'

'You have changed your tune.'

'Yeah, I guess I have. Anyway, let's not talk about her. What can I do for you?'

'You did ask me to let you know what happened, didn't you?'

'Oh God, yeah, I did, didn't I? But you could have called. I didn't expect you to come all the way over here especially. Do you want to come in?'

'Actually, I came over here because there are some woods the other side of Tinton. I've walked the dog there before, and I can assure you it's a great place to walk for an hour or two.'

Slater thought for a second. The way he was feeling he wasn't sure he wanted company. He looked over her head at the weather. Although it was a chilly morning, the sun was breaking through, and he knew the fresh air would probably do him good.

'You say you've got the dog with you?'

'He's in the back of the car, that's why I won't come in.'

'What sort of dog is it?'

'A spaniel. He's quite friendly.'

'Is this after you cried your eyes out? You did say that was the first thing you said you would do, didn't you?'

Her smile widened.

'I'm not telling you what happened unless you come for a walk.'

Slater thought some more.

'And you reckon this is good therapy, right?' he asked.

'It always works for me.'

'Will it work for me?'

'Why don't you come and find out? I might even let you buy that breakfast you owe me.'

Slater remembered his resolution about avoiding women, set just a few minutes ago.

'It'll be a bit late for breakfast.'

'Alright, you can buy me brunch, or lunch, or whatever you want to call it.'

'What about the dog?'

'Oh, he won't mind. You can buy him lunch, too, if you like.'

Slater made his mind up. After all, he hadn't said anything about avoiding spaniels, had he?

THE END

THE JOFFE BOOKS STORY

We began in 2014 when Jasper agreed to publish his mum's much-rejected romance novel and it became a bestseller.

Since then we've grown into the largest independent publisher in the UK. We're extremely proud to publish some of the very best writers in the world, including Joy Ellis, Faith Martin, Caro Ramsay, Helen Forrester, Simon Brett and Robert Goddard. Everyone at Joffe Books loves reading and we never forget that it all begins with the magic of an author telling a story.

We are proud to publish talented first-time authors, as well as established writers whose books we love introducing to a new generation of readers.

We won Trade Publisher of the Year at the Independent Publishing Awards in 2023. We have been shortlisted for Independent Publisher of the Year at the British Book Awards for the last four years, and were shortlisted for the Diversity and Inclusivity Award at the 2022 Independent Publishing Awards. In 2023 we were shortlisted for Publisher of the Year at the RNA Industry Awards.

We built this company with your help, and we love to hear from you, so please email us about absolutely anything bookish at feedback@joffebooks.com

If you want to receive free books every Friday and hear about all our new releases, join our mailing list: www.joffebooks.com/contact

And when you tell your friends about us, just remember: it's pronounced Joffe as in coffee or toffee!

Printed in Dunstable, United Kingdom

70855534R00129